The Black Chair

PHIL CARRADICE

Gomer

Published in 2009 by Pont Books, an imprint of
Gomer Press, Llandysul, Ceredigion, SA44 4JL

Reprinted – 2017

ISBN 978 1 84323 978 9

A CIP record for this title is available from the British Library.

This book is published with the financial support of the
Welsh Books Council.

Printed and bound in Wales at
Gomer Press, Llandysul, Ceredigion

Chapter One

Danny hesitated, unsure and more than a little afraid, outside the red-brick hall. He watched as the crowds pushed past – men in dark suits and bowler hats, women in light, brightly-coloured summer dresses, even the odd soldier or sailor in their khaki and blue uniforms. He could hear the excited grumble of their voices as they moved around him . . . but everyone spoke in rapid Welsh and he could understand barely a word of what they were saying.

His leg hurt and, in an effort to ease the pain, he pushed the weight onto his right foot. The crutches cut into his armpits, his groin burned like fire and he guessed that the wound had begun to weep again. No matter, he would have to endure it.

'*Ydych chi'n mynd mewn*?' said a voice from alongside him. 'Are you going in?'

Danny looked around. A short dark man in a straw boater was staring at him, gazing intently into his eyes. Danny nodded. 'When the rush eases off. Best keep out of too much trouble, I reckon.' He pointed to his leg.

'A Blighty wound?' asked the man.

Danny raised his arm to show the wound stripes on his sleeve. 'German machine gun at Passchendaele. Three bullets in the thigh and groin. I was lucky – they missed all the vital bits.'

The stranger grinned and stretched out his hand. 'Lloyd, Thomas Lloyd, from Caernarfon. The South African campaign – the Boer War – that was my war. I'm too old for this one. All I can do now is read the news in the papers and wish you boys all the best of luck. I'm glad to meet you.'

Awkwardly, adjusting the crutches beneath his arms, Danny shook his hand.

From inside the hall he could sense the atmosphere of tense excitement. 'I don't suppose I'll understand much of what's going on,' shrugged Danny. 'I speak no Welsh. I'm from the south, from Treorchy in the Rhondda – it's a mining town.'

Lloyd nodded. 'I know where it is, boy. You're a collier?'

'I was, until I joined up.' Danny paused and stared down at the distinctive braiding on his uniform sleeve. 'For the past year I've been a soldier. Private Daniel Jones, Royal Welch Fusiliers – at your service.' He tried to stand to attention but the pain in his thigh was too intense, and he staggered backwards.

'Careful, boy,' said Lloyd, steadying him. 'We don't want you injuring yourself again, do we?'

Danny shrugged and managed to straighten himself.

Thomas Lloyd inched closer. 'What's it really like out there? I know the papers keep talking about victory after victory but here we are, 1917, and the end of the war seems no closer than when it started three years ago. The casualty lists just keep getting bigger and bigger.'

'What do you expect,' Danny said, 'when generals think the only way to defeat the Germans is by throwing more and more men against fixed machine guns and artillery? This war is different from any other that's ever been fought. Those weapons are deadly and nobody's got any idea how to get the better of them.'

He stopped, as if realising he had gone too far – after all he didn't know this man. Thomas Lloyd could have been a policeman or a government official. He'd heard that there were people like that, paid to report on what soldiers back from France and the Western Front were saying about the war.

'So what are you doing here in Birkenhead at the National Eisteddfod of Wales? It's a long way from Treorchy, particularly for a man on crutches. And if, as you say, you speak no Welsh . . .'

Danny glanced towards the entrance doors of the Eisteddfod hall where people still flooded and jostled their way up the steps. 'I made a promise to a friend, that's all. He wasn't able to be here today. I was.'

Thomas Lloyd frowned, puzzled.

Suddenly, Danny turned back to face him. 'Look, I know I have no right to ask you this but you're from north Wales, aren't you? You speak Welsh, at any rate. Do you think you could help me? I mean stand with me, tell me what's going on – when I finally do manage to get in?'

Thomas Lloyd nodded and took the young man's arm. 'Of course. It isn't every day you get to see the Chairing of the Bard, is it? You understand what that means?'

Danny nodded. 'Chairing the Bard? It's when they announce the champion poet for the year. It's a bit like crowning him, I suppose, except that he gets a fancy chair rather than a crown. Yes, Ellis told me all about the Eisteddfod.' He stopped. 'It's just that I hadn't expected it to be so – so big. There must be three or four hundred people in there.'

'More like six or seven, if you ask me,' nodded Lloyd. 'The National Eisteddfod is a great experience, boy, and we have such a lovely day for it. We must make sure you enjoy it.'

Danny stared up at the sky. The day was beautifully warm, only the occasional wispy cloud breaking the expanse of blue. From the river behind them came the sudden blast of a ship's siren. It was quickly followed by several others. The country had been at war with Germany for over three years and work on the Mersey, in the ports of Birkenhead and Liverpool, seemed never to stop.

'We have our eisteddfodau down south, you know,' said Danny. 'All the chapels hold one every year, a competition for music and things. But this one is special, isn't it? The National – and the Chair – well, it's what every Welsh poet wants to win. That's what my friend said.'

Thomas Lloyd nodded. 'Your friend was right. But

look, it's not so crowded now. Let's get inside.' Carefully he led Danny into the hall. The heat was like a solid wall, and Danny immediately felt the sweat breaking out across his chest. At first he saw only a mass of figures and faces. Everyone stood shoulder to shoulder and it seemed as if there wasn't an inch of spare space. Then, noticing his uniform and crutches, people quickly moved aside to allow him to stand in comfort.

They found a place halfway down the hall and Lloyd explained what was happening. He pointed out the white-robed Druids as they filed onto the platform until, eventually, the Chairing ceremony began. It was the event everyone was waiting for.

When the moment came, a blanketing hush fell across the hall. Danny gasped as he heard the name of the winner – Fleur-de-lis. He had wanted it, expected it even, but the confirmation still came as a shock. He felt a pain in his chest and knew that Ellis had been right.

When the Adjudicator asked for the winning poet to stand up and be recognised, nobody moved. Should I say something, Danny thought, should I tell them?

Before he could say anything, a man, black-suited and sombre, slipped out from the back of the stage. He spoke quietly into the Archdruid's ear. The two men seemed to be whispering for hours, Danny felt, but later he knew their conversation had taken only moments. Then the Archdruid stepped forward and began to speak in Welsh. There was a combined intake of breath as everyone in the hall gasped at precisely the same moment.

Danny, though he could not understand one word, felt a wave of sadness ripple through the audience and he grabbed urgently at Thomas Lloyd's arm. 'What's happening? What's happening?'

Lloyd put his hand over Danny's clutching fingers and squeezed. His eyes were full of tears. 'They're saying they can't go on with the ceremony, not after what's taken place. It wouldn't be right. But look - the Chair - look. They're covering it in black cloth. The winner, our Bard, has been killed in the fighting in France. Hedd Wyn, that's his bardic name - Fleur-de-lis is the pseudonym he used. He's won the Chair – the Black Chair.'

Danny did not reply. He didn't know whether to laugh or cry. He'd done it; Ellis had done it, just as he said he would all those weeks ago at Ypres. Danny's mouth was dry and his stomach felt huge. Eventually, however, he managed to find his voice again. 'I knew it, I knew he'd win. Hedd Wyn? He was my friend. That's why I'm here today. I told him I'd come if he couldn't; I told him I'd be here.'

Thomas Lloyd stared at him, puzzled. 'Let's go and find ourselves a cup of tea,' he said. 'Then you can tell me all about it.'

They pushed their way out of the hall, Danny letting the older man lead him out and along the pavement. Almost before he knew what was happening, he found himself seated at one of the tables in a small tea-shop. Apart from them, the place was empty.

'Hedd Wyn,' Danny whispered as Lloyd poured out

the tea. 'His real name was Ellis Evans.' He stopped and ladled sugar into his cup but did not even try to drink. 'If it wasn't for Ellis, I wouldn't even be here today,' he continued. He began to stir his tea, the spoon circling and clinking against the china rim.

After a few moments, Lloyd reached out and laid a restraining hand over Danny's. 'Do you want to tell me about it?'

Danny shrugged. 'It's a long story.'

'I've got time,' said Lloyd. 'My train doesn't leave for a couple of hours. And if I miss it then I'm sure Caernarfon will wait a while longer.'

Danny sat back in his seat, pushing his crutches out of sight beneath the table. It was, indeed, a long story but it was one that needed to be told. The wounds in his left leg burned furiously, throbbing as if somebody was trying to pull a strand of barbed wire out of his thigh, and for a moment he was back in the mud and filth of Flanders. 'I'll tell you,' he said, blinking away a sudden wetness from his eyes. 'If you're ready?'

Thomas Lloyd opened his arms. 'I'm ready,' he said. 'Tell me.'

Chapter Two

'I don't understand,' said Angharad. 'Why do you have to go?'

The plea in her voice was desperate and Danny knew that she was close to tears. Yet he could not help himself – or her.

'You're far too young,' Angharad continued. 'They're not taking boys yet, are they?'

'I'm not a boy!' Danny shouted, whirling around to face her.

They were high up on the hillside above the valley. It was early evening in the little town below and already there were clusters of lights, bright as glow-worms, on the street corners. As far as his eyes could see, houses lined the hillsides and the valley floor. Row upon row of terraces stretched away into the distance, one town or village running into the next, until it seemed as if the whole of the Rhondda was just one continuous line of bricks and mortar.

Here and there the metal winding gear of a colliery or the low squat bulk of a chapel broke the unity. They looked like stubby fingers, Danny thought, reaching up above the regular lines and knuckles of the streets – the mines for work, the chapels for religion and,

12

in between them all, dozens upon dozens of public houses.

'It's almost like a painting, isn't it?' he said. 'From up here, it all looks so peaceful and calm.'

Angharad glared at him. 'Don't change the subject. Tell me why you think you have to join the army. You're too young; they'll never take you. Why, Danny, why?'

He turned back to stare out over the valley. 'Because I have to,' he said. Down there, it was all dust and grime, the smoke from the collieries and goods yards coiling around the slag heaps and the streets of the town. Only up here, on the hills, in the sunlight, could he feel clean and fresh.

'Because I have to,' he repeated. 'Joining the army is probably the best chance I'll ever have. I don't want to spend my life underground, Annie. I want to see something of the world. And anyway, I'm almost sixteen. They need every soldier they can get. They'll take me.'

Angharad grabbed at his arm. 'They'll call for you soon enough, Danny. My father was saying, only last night, that the Government will be introducing conscription in a few months. That means everyone will have to join the army or the navy sooner or later. If you're that desperate to go and fight, why not wait until they call you up?'

Danny shook his head. 'That's why I want to join up now. Next year we'll all have to register. They'll make me wait another two years and by then it'll all be over.' He paused. 'Besides, I don't want to be called up. I want to be a volunteer.'

He grinned and caught her by the waist, spinning her around. 'Remember, it's an extra shilling a day as a volunteer.'

Angharad was not to be placated. She broke free from his grip, her dark hair flying around her shoulders. 'It's nothing to laugh at. You've got a steady job in the pit; you're earning good money. Why put yourself in danger?'

Danny sniffed. 'I put myself in danger every time I step into the cage to go underground. Like I told you, I don't want to spend the next thirty years scrabbling around in the dust and dirt, knowing that a ton of rock could fall on top of my head any second. Or crawling through headings two feet high, working up to my knees in freezing water.' He reached out and took her hands. 'Look, this war's been going on for almost two years now . . .'

'And you think that it's going to be finished a lot quicker just by you joining the army? That's mighty big of you, Danny.'

He grinned at her, the lop-sided smile that she loved so much. Then he shrugged. 'If everybody thought like that, there'd be nobody to fight, would there?'

'And would that be such a bad idea?' whispered Angharad.

'Of course it would,' he responded. 'We all have to do our duty. Somebody's got to stop the Kaiser – if he defeats us in France then God only knows what he'll do next.'

Angharad did not reply. A sudden chill blew in with the dusk and she felt frightened. She shivered as the tears came to her eyes.

'What is it?' Danny asked. 'What's wrong?'

She shrugged. 'I'm just scared. Scared something is going to happen to you. I really don't want you to do this, Danny. I hope they don't take you.'

He took her in his arms and held her. He could feel her heart beating against his chest. 'I know you're frightened. But I'll come back, believe me. I'll come back and then we'll be married, like we planned. I'll get a job – not down the mines, somewhere above ground where I can breathe the air, somewhere that's fresh and clean. Maybe I'll be a farmer. Or a keeper on one of the big estates over Mountain Ash way. Just not coal mining.'

He stared into her eyes. 'I love you, Annie. But I have to do this. Don't make it hard . . . please. I have to.'

They went slowly, carefully, down the hillside in the dark and Angharad could not argue or plead any more. But the fear remained, solid as a fist in her belly, and nothing would make it go away.

*

Danny was at the town's Taff Vale station early the following day, ready for the first train down the valley to Cardiff. He had not told his mother what he was intending to do but had crept out at first light, before she was properly awake.

'Danny, is that you?' she called as his foot hit the creaking stair close to the bottom. She was half asleep and disorientated.

'Go back to sleep, Mam. It's early yet.'

'Good boy,' she mumbled and Danny knew she would drift back in a few minutes.

He grabbed a piece of bread off the end of a loaf and took a quick drink before ghosting out of the door, closing it silently behind him. He set off down the deserted street. There would be time enough for explanations later. A small knot of apprehension began to flutter in his stomach. He was scared but excited at the same time.

*

The train rattled and belched its way down the Rhondda Fach. Each successive town looked exactly the same to Danny, the same pitheads, the same Miners' Institutes. Even the groups of old men, already standing on the street corners, looked the same. Everything was tight and close and compact.

Only when they reached the high-level platform at Pontypridd did the valley finally open up. The flat plain of Cardiff and the Vale of Glamorgan lay ahead.

*

Danny let down the carriage window, easing back the leather strap so that the glass caught and held halfway down. He leaned out, narrowing his eyes against the smuts and smoke of the engine, and tried to catch his first glimpse of the Bristol Channel.

16

'Forget it, son,' said an old man from the opposite seat. 'You'll not see the sea, not till we get to Cardiff. And that's another half an hour away, at least.'

Danny slumped back onto the hard slats of the third-class seat and studied his companion. From the criss-crossing of tiny blue scars along his cheek and forehead, the man was obviously an old miner. He saw Danny staring at him and glared back.

'Day out, is it?' he asked when he had studied Danny for long enough.

Danny smiled. In his best blazer and flannels – his dead father's blazer and flannels – he could easily have been heading off for a day at Barry Island or Penarth. He shook his head. 'I'm going to Cardiff to enlist, to join the army and fight in the war.'

The old miner snorted. 'Get on with you, boy. You're no more than a lad. They'll never take you in the army; they don't want babies – not yet, at any rate. Them Germans are professional soldiers. They've been leading our boys a merry dance for two years now – it needs real fighters, real men, to take them on. Take my advice and get on home to your mam.'

He paused, pulled out the stump of an old black pipe and slowly shook his head. 'I don't know, young pups with no more sense than they were born with.'

They lapsed into a sullen silence, the old man sucking on his pipe, Danny sitting resentfully in his corner. The man's comments had unsettled him. What if he was right? What if Angharad was right, too, and they refused to take

17

him? He did not know what he would do. He worried at the notion until, finally, the train pulled into Queen Street station.

The moment the train juddered to a halt, Danny jumped to his feet and was out through the door before the old man had time to speak again. He set off down the platform, pushing his way through the crowds, and only at the ticket barrier did he pause to stare back. The old miner was leaning casually out of the carriage window. He saw Danny looking and slowly, deliberately, shook his head.

It didn't matter. Danny was in the city now and he was excited and expectant. A whole new world lay before him.

When he reached the recruiting office, he found the place empty. No wonder the Government was thinking of introducing conscription, he told himself, remembering the wild excitement of August 1914. Back then, when the papers first broke the news of war between Britain and Germany, thousands had rushed to join the army and women had even handed out white feathers to men not in uniform.

He remembered the recruiting drive they had held in Treorchy during that first month of the war. A band, followed by soldiers in scarlet uniform – and a recruiting sergeant, an old sweat who had served his time in India or somewhere equally exotic – had marched up the street, calling for men to take the King's shilling and help deliver the world from the army of the German Kaiser. Danny had stood with his father and mother and watched, feeling the excitement driving through his body. He was caught up in the glory and the splendour of it all and found himself inching forward to the front of the crowd.

'Stop him, John,' his mother had said, guessing what was in his mind.

His father smiled at him with his watering blue eyes, his wasting body racked by coal dust. 'Wait, boy,' he had said. 'Wait a while longer.'

So he had stood there, watching and listening as the band blared and marched on. He had never forgotten the pomp and ceremony of that band or the soldiers. But that was over a year ago and now things seemed to be very different. He pushed the thoughts out of his head and went in through the office door.

'What can I do for you, son?' A tall regimental sergeant major with a bristling moustache and carrying a swagger stick under his arm was glaring at him.

'I want to join the army,' Danny said.

The RSM studied him through narrowed eyes and then settled himself behind a long trestle table. 'How old are you?'

'Eighteen, sir.'

The RSM sniffed. 'Date of birth?'

The question caught Danny by surprise. 'Er, December, 12 December 1899.'

The sergeant major stood, drew himself up to his full height and came carefully around the table. He tapped Danny on the chest with his stick.

'Do me a favour, son. Take a walk around the park and consider your answer. I think you'll find that date is out by a couple of years.' He winked at Danny. 'Come back in half an hour and be two or three years older, eh lad?'

Danny stumbled out through the doorway, cursing himself for his stupidity. He had always known he'd have to lie about his age but he hadn't expected to give his date of birth like that. He needed to get the date straight in his head. Thank God the sergeant major seemed to be on his side.

He was back at the recruiting office within an hour, this time with his fictional date of birth fixed firmly in his brain. The RSM smiled at him and nodded his approval. Along with three other young men Danny was taken to a small back room and sworn in. The sergeant major presented him with a brand new shilling piece and he signed his name at the bottom of a parchment scroll.

'Welcome to the army, boy,' said the RSM. 'We'll make a man of you – you'll have the time of your life. Now go on home; we'll be in touch.'

Danny was confused. Go home? Why? 'But I thought I'd joined the army,' he said.

The RSM smiled grimly and propelled him towards the office door. 'You have, boy, you have. But we don't want you here and now, just like that. That ain't how it works. There's procedures to follow – you'll find the army is full of procedures, lad. We got to have our systems, now don't we? You'll have to have a medical, for a start, to check you're fit and healthy enough to serve King and Country. And then you'll have to wait until a new detachment is formed. That could take several weeks, maybe even longer.'

He smiled at the young man's downcast face. 'Don't worry, boy; we'll be calling for you soon enough. We're going to need every man we can lay our hands on before this war is over. Go on home and wait.'

*

At least Angharad was pleased to see him when he called at her house that night. Like Danny, she had thought he would be marched off to a training camp that very day. 'What did your mother say when you told her?' she asked.

Danny shrugged. 'Nothing. You know what she's like these days. Since Dad died she's got no interest in anything. I suppose, in one way, she's relieved – at least I'll be one less mouth to feed. And I'll send her money from my army pay.'

They walked up the hill, out of town, to their favourite place on the mountain. Danny put his arm around Angharad's waist and she laid her head on his shoulder. 'I wish you weren't going,' she said.

Danny sighed and prepared himself for another argument.

Before he could speak, Angharad pulled away and laid her finger on his lips. 'I'm not going to argue with you. I don't like what you've done and I don't agree with it. But I accept it. We've only got a short time before they take you away; let's enjoy it while we can.'

*

As it happened, Angharad was wrong. The days stretched out into weeks, then months. Christmas came and went and still there was no word from Cardiff. It was a strange period, one of anxiety on the one hand and intense happiness on the other. They both knew that eventually the call would come and for Danny, at least, there was an overwhelming desire to get things started. He had made his decision; and, no matter what he felt for Angharad, waiting for things to happen was hard.

'I think they've forgotten me,' he complained as they sat, one warm spring night, on their hill overlooking the town. 'They must have realised I lied about my age.'

'Good,' said Angharad. 'Now that conscription's come in, you'll have to wait a while longer. And who knows? In a few months the war could be over.'

'Maybe.' He tried to smile at her, knowing how desperately she wanted him to stay. Yet despite everything, despite her hopes and his words, he knew that the army had not forgotten him. Sooner or later they would send for him.

*

It was almost nine months after his trip to Cardiff that Danny's call to duty finally arrived. One wet August morning a brown envelope fell through the letterbox. Inside was a flimsy piece of paper ordering him to report to the barracks the following week.

Angharad went with him to the station and stood on the platform as steam and smoke billowed around the carriages. He tried to make her smile but she could not respond and finally they fell into an uneasy silence. For almost ten minutes they stood there, not speaking or looking at each other until, finally, the guard blew his whistle and Danny climbed, almost gratefully, into his compartment.

'Take care of yourself,' he said. 'I'll write every week and let you know what I'm doing.' He reached out through the open window and kissed her. She clung to him, desperate now that the parting was upon them, and he saw the sadness in her eyes. He was suddenly guilty, knowing his excitement must be clearly visible to her. He was setting off on an adventure, a journey like he had only ever dreamed about. He wanted to be away and wished that the train would start.

'Good luck,' Angharad breathed into his ear, winding her fingers around his and holding on tightly. 'I'll never stop thinking about you. Just make sure you come back.'

He smiled at her. Then, with a lurch and a grinding of metal, the train started to move. A cloud of smoke rolled down the platform, cloaking Angharad and the familiar outline of the station buildings. Danny could taste acrid bitterness and felt himself being pulled away from her. For a few moments her fingers held on tightly and then, at last, their grip was broken.

He had one final glimpse of Angharad standing alone and lonely on the platform. Then she was lost to view as the train gathered speed and pulled away down the valley. Danny closed the window and sat back on the seat. It had begun.

Chapter Three

The training was hard. The Royal Welch Fusiliers was an old regiment and its officers prided themselves on the quality of their soldiers. From early morning till late in the evening the new recruits were marched and chased around the camp until they were dizzy and reeling. They had hardly a moment to themselves, every second of the day taken up with the intricate business of learning how to be soldiers.

As the days and weeks advanced, they learned how to drill and how to dig trenches. They learned how to clean and fire their rifles. They made furious bayonet charges across the instruction ground, frightening themselves with the ferocity of their screams as they plunged their weapons into the waiting sacks of sawdust.

'Six inches, just six inches,' the instructors repeated. 'That's all you need. Any more than that, your bayonet will get stuck and you'll never pull it out. Give him a couple of inches of good British steel and then a quarter turn to the right. That'll finish off any Hun who gets in your way, makes a fatal wound immortal!'

Danny's stomach always turned over at that. The bloodthirsty comments of the instructors felt worse than the actual bayonet charges themselves. Young as he was, he couldn't help noticing that the more removed such men were from the fighting, the more determined and vicious they became.

When the recruits were not training, they were sent on fatigue parties, cleaning and sweeping the barracks and the parade ground until there wasn't one piece of rubbish to be found in the entire camp. And almost from the beginning, Danny realised that he was not a natural soldier.

'I've got a good enough sense of rhythm,' he wrote to Angharad one night, 'but I seem to have trouble marching in time with other men, moving together as one body – if you see what I mean.' He did not tell her how the drill instructors bellowed at him constantly.

From the barracks at Cardiff, Danny and his detachment had been sent north, to the battalion base at Wrexham. They joined other recruits and set about casting out the last remnants of civilian life. Week after week the training continued and Danny knew that his lack of ability was beginning to cause resentment amongst some of the other recruits. He could do nothing about it. The harder he tried, the worse things became. He was out of his depth and floundering.

He tried hard not to tell Angharad how he was feeling but sometimes it was difficult to keep the resentment out of his letters. 'I hate it here,' he wrote. 'Everything is controlled by rules. We have rules for going to bed, rules for getting up in the morning, rules for washing clothes – even rules for going to chapel. I'm sure it will be a lot better when we finish our training but at the moment I just wish I'd listened to you and stayed at home.'

*

Christmas was a strange time, one of loneliness and longing. For most of them it was the first time they had spent Christmas away from their families and, as the festive season approached, a wave of home sickness seemed to sweep through the ranks.

The drill sergeants and corporals tried to keep their minds on other things with a round of back-breaking route marches. On Christmas Eve the Padre held a service in the church and the tiny building was full to overcrowding as disconsolate, lonely men crowded in to sing the hymns and carols that reminded them of home.

Afterwards Danny sat on his bunk, reading and re-reading Angharad's letters.

*

New Year brought a change of billet and a new set of companions, though the prospect of heading out to France and fighting on the Western Front seemed further away than ever. Every spare second, Danny sat in the hut and wrote scribbled notes to Angharad.

'It's hard to believe how long it is since we first talked about me joining up,' he wrote to her one evening. 'Please God all this marching and training will be over soon.

Then we can get on with being soldiers at war. The way I look at it, the sooner we go into battle and get the job done, the sooner I'll be home with you.'

He sat back and thought about what he'd written. Should he really send thoughts like that to Angharad? At that moment a dark shadow fell across the page and a hand swept down to seize his stub of candle.

'You've had this long enough, little boy,' said a voice. 'I've got a letter to write; you go and practise how to march. That way you won't get us all into trouble with the drill corporal.'

Danny looked up into the cold, grey eyes of Frank Mitchell. From the first, the man had taken a dislike to him and never missed a chance to humiliate him, pushing him out of the way in the meal queue, deliberately barging into him on their morning cross-country run, making him the butt of all his crude and vicious jokes.

'I haven't finished,' Danny said. 'Give that back.' He rose to his feet and reached out for the candle. It was a mistake; he was off balance and vulnerable. Mitchell swung around, punching him hard on the jaw. Danny's head jerked backwards and he fell heavily to the floor. His head swam and he scrabbled with his hands to push himself into a sitting position. He was aware of the older man towering above him.

'You've had this coming! Perhaps this will teach you to be a soldier.' He drew back his foot, Danny saw the huge hobnailed boot begin to swing, closed his eyes and tried to roll away.

But the kick never came and the next second his aggressor was lying face down on the hut floor.

A tall man with fists the size of shovels was standing over Frank Mitchell. His voice was surprisingly light but there was no mistaking its power and control. 'Leave the boy alone. He is doing his best, just like the rest of us. Maybe you could learn a little compassion. That would be a good thing for you to start with, wouldn't it?'

The man spoke slowly, his accent and deliberate choice of words telling Danny that English was probably not his first language. At last he turned away from Frank, swung around and helped Danny to his feet.

'I'm Ellis,' he said, 'Ellis Evans. Come on, let's go to the canteen and find a good mug of tea.'

Danny smiled weakly and followed him out through the door. Frank Mitchell limped unsteadily to his bunk and glared after them.

The canteen was located in a tin hut at the end of a row of other tin huts, all exactly the same size and design. It was run by local volunteers, women who tried to provide a degree of comfort for men a long way from their homes. When Danny and Ellis entered, the place was almost full but they managed to find a table and sat down.

Danny looked gratefully at Ellis. Till now he had barely noticed him, a tall, quiet man he had first seen when he joined the unit at Wrexham.

'How's the jaw?'

Danny felt gingerly at his chin. 'Sore. Thanks for what you did or it would have been a lot worse.'

Ellis shrugged and stirred sugar into his tea. His big hands seemed to cover not only the cup but half the table as well. 'I hate bullies; I hate fighting. I'd much rather be back home looking after my sheep.'

'Are you a farmer?'

'Yes,' said Ellis. 'At Trawsfynydd – do you know where that is?'

Danny frowned. 'I think so – in north Wales? By Snowdon?'

Ellis smiled. 'Not far away. I live on a farm with my brothers. We tend the sheep. That's my work.'

'I was a miner before I joined up,' said Danny, 'but I don't ever want to go back to it!'

'I worked in the mines for a few months – down in the south. But not for long. I need to feel the wind on my face. So I came back to Trawsfynydd. I did like the singing in your chapels, though. Hymns are really poetry, poems set to music. Do you like poetry?'

'Not really. There's not much call for it in a coal mine!'

'I write poetry,' said the older man.

'Really? You're a proper poet, someone who writes books?'

Ellis laughed. 'I've won at several eisteddfodau. I write in *cynghanedd*. Strict metre. Do you know what that means?'

Danny shook his head. He hadn't met anyone like this before.

Ellis smiled and took a sip of tea. 'It is hard to understand but I will try to explain.'

Much of the explanation about rhymes and consonants went straight over Danny's head but he was spellbound by the man's passion for his writing, and intrigued when Ellis explained that poets used a bardic name for eisteddfod competitions.

'Mine's *Hedd Wyn*. It means *Shining Peace*.'

Danny grinned. 'Do you want me to call you Hedd Wyn?' he asked.

'Ellis will be fine.'

It was so odd, to be sitting there with a real live poet, Danny thought, someone who used words to make pictures and ideas come alive in your head. He'd always thought writing poetry was something people did in universities or colleges. It was hard to accept that this tough Welsh shepherd could also handle something as delicate as a line of verse.

For a long time they sat in the canteen, just talking. 'We'd better be getting back,' said Ellis at last.

'I'll never get used to army discipline,' Danny sighed.

He was reluctant to go and Ellis sensed it. 'Don't worry about Frank. He won't bother you.'

'It isn't that. It's just that this is the first sensible conversation I've had in weeks.'

'We can talk again. Maybe I'll even read you some of my poetry.'

'Will you? Honestly?'

'Of course. Just tell me one thing – how old are you, Danny? Really.'

Danny glanced quickly around. Nobody was listening.

'You won't tell anyone, will you? I was seventeen a few weeks ago.'

Ellis shook his head and a wicked twinkle appeared in his eyes. 'It's past your bedtime then.'

If Frank Mitchell had said it, Danny would have bristled with anger. But he knew that Ellis was just pulling his leg. They laughed and, together, went out into the night.

*

It was a strange friendship. They sat together at mealtimes and worked side by side on the rifle range. Gradually Danny told the older man about his dreams and ambitions and about Angharad. For his part, Ellis listened wisely, letting the boy talk.

And Danny's confidence grew. Somehow the drills became simpler, the catcalls of the instructors easier to take. On the rifle range his shooting improved. Even his uniform, which had previously sat on his body like an unmade bed, seemed to fit better.

'Tell me about your farm?' Danny said one day.

They were stationed, part of a small squad, on a gorse-covered hillside, high above a cart track, taking part in what Sergeant Jenkins, the platoon NCO, had called 'a combat exercise'. The enemy, another squad, was due to come down the track in a few minutes and they had laid their ambush carefully. Now all they could do was sit and wait.

'My farm?' said Ellis. 'It's not even a farm, really, just a smallholding. It's called Yr Ysgwrn and lies about a mile outside the village. But when you're out on the hills and there's not another living soul to be seen, anywhere, it feels like you could reach out and touch God's hand.'

He stared up at the sky. 'I tell you, Danny, there's nowhere like that farm. The mountains lie all around you – the Berwyns, Cader Idris, Snowdon. The views are spectacular. And the air, boy, well, it's so pure, it's like water.'

Before Danny could reply, the sound of voices echoed along the cart track – the 'enemy' patrol was coming. Ellis clambered to his knees and waved to the other section on the far side of the valley. There was a brief answering wave, then all was still once more.

The voices from below grew steadily louder. Danny recognised Frank Mitchell's arrogant tones and smiled to himself. Was he going to be in for a surprise!

Within two minutes Mitchell and his squad appeared on the path, rifles slung carelessly across their shoulders, hats pushed back on their heads. One of them even had a cigarette stub dangling from the corner of his mouth. They could have been out for a Sunday morning stroll.

'Now!' Ellis shouted.

Screaming like banshees, they fell over the brow and down the hill, onto the unsuspecting patrol before it had time to run or even react. It was over in seconds. The smoker hadn't even had time to take the Woodbine from his mouth. Surprise was complete and the whole party simply threw up their hands in surrender.

When Ellis delivered them to Sergeant Jenkins, Mitchell glared at him but knew better than to open his mouth. 'Good job, well executed,' nodded the Sergeant, gesturing the captured men to their feet. 'Work like that when we get out to France and we'll soon have the Hun on the run.'

They began to walk back towards camp, all of them relaxing in the sunshine.

'We might have to think about getting you a stripe, Private Evans,' the Sergeant announced. 'Corporal, how does that sound?'

'Not for me, thank you, Sergeant,' said Ellis. 'All I want is to get this war over and then go back home to my family. Give the stripe to Private Mitchell or someone who wants it.'

Jenkins frowned at him, then shook his head in disbelief. 'I'll never understand you make-believe soldiers. Don't you want to get on in this man's army?'

He strolled on ahead of them, casually lighting his pipe and still shaking his head. Danny looked across at Ellis and raised his eyebrows. 'Frank? Give Frank a stripe? You didn't mean that, did you? I can't imagine anything worse.'

'Oh, Frank will get his promotion, sooner or later. He's been sucking up to Sergeant Jenkins for weeks now. *Seboni,* we would say in Welsh. He may not get it for a while, not after today's performance, but he'll get it eventually.' He grinned at Danny. 'Anyway, forget promotion and corporal's stripes. Look, can you see that buzzard over there, standing on the telegraph pole? Now that's a sight worth remembering.'

They walked on. Ellis was already deep in thought, conjuring words and pictures in his head. Danny was content. He knew that in some ways he had never been happier.

Chapter Four

At last the day came when they finally finished their basic training. Danny was proud of what he had achieved; proud of his newfound skill with rifle and bayonet; proud of his uniform with the distinctive braiding and the flash at the back of the tunic collar, the unique fan-shaped black ribbons that only the Royal Welch Fusiliers could wear. Now, at last, he felt ready to fight. 'Where do you think they'll send us?'

He and Ellis were sitting in the canteen with the rest of the platoon, waiting to learn what would happen next. Rumour was rife but the one thing everyone expected was to be sent out to France very, very soon.

'I heard that the last lot to finish training went straight from here to the Battle of the Somme,' said Bert Phillips. 'Most of them were killed on the first day.'

Bert was a short, stocky lad from Birmingham. He and his friend Tudor were inseparable. And now Tudor, sitting opposite, was nodding in agreement.

'It's true,' he said. 'I heard it from one of the drill instructors.'

Ellis shook his head. 'The Regiment wasn't involved on the first day of the Somme,' he said quietly. 'The Fusiliers didn't go into action until they attacked Mametz Wood, five or six days later. It's all rumour.'

'Well rumour or not,' said Frank Mitchell, 'I was talking to Sergeant Jenkins the other day and he said we'd be off to the Somme inside a week.'

As Ellis had predicted, Frank had got his stripe. He was now Lance Corporal Frank Mitchell and loved nothing more than to lord his position of authority over the platoon. He kept clear of Ellis, however, remembering only too well what had happened the one time he had pushed the quiet shepherd too far.

'You really think they'll send us to the Somme?' asked Danny, hardly able to keep the excitement out of his voice. 'Or maybe to Ypres.'

Ellis shook his head. 'I doubt if even Field Marshal Haig is foolish enough to send part-trained, untried men to fight against experienced soldiers. I imagine we'll be sent somewhere fairly safe first off, on garrison duties for a few months. After that we'll be sent to France.'

Bert Phillips pushed back his chair and walked to the door. It was raining heavily and the rattling on the roof was as loud as a volley of rifle bullets. 'I don't care where they send us, as long as we get away from this damned Tin Town. I never want to see another tin hut as long as I live.'

*

Ellis was right. Early the following day Bert and Tudor came racing into the barracks, eyes glittering. Bert was dragging another soldier behind him. Danny recognised

Tommy Thomas, Tommy Twice as they called him, another Rhondda man.

'We've had our orders,' Bert shouted. 'Tommy Twice saw them in the orderly office. Tell them, Tommy.'

Tommy Twice was a small man. He'd been a clerk in one of the Rhondda coal mines before the war and now spent most of his time working in the company office. He smiled, weakly, and spread his hands. 'It was on a piece of paper in the office. It had our battalion number on the top and then it said L'pol. That's where we're headed, L'pol.'

Bert and Tudor began dancing around the hut, chanting 'L'pol, L'pol' at the tops of their voices. Eventually they collapsed, exhausted, onto their bunks.

'L'pol, where do you reckon that is?' asked Tudor. 'I bet it's somewhere in Belgium or France, somewhere close to Ypres. It sounds French, doesn't it?'

'Oh, it's close to Ypres, all right,' said Frank Mitchell, coming in through the door. 'About four hundred miles close. It means Liverpool, you idiots. We're not going to France or Belgium. We're off to Litherland Camp in Liverpool.'

*

They quickly established themselves in yet another Tin Town close to the outskirts of Liverpool. And there, once more, they began the round of never-ending bayonet charges and trench digging. At times it seemed as if their basic training had never stopped.

'I thought my hands were calloused down the mine,' sighed Danny, massaging his palms. 'I've got blisters on top of blisters here.'

They were digging trenches at the edge of the parade ground, the third day running that they had drawn this hated task. Forget bayonet charges and close order marching, they were told, learning to dig proper trenches was the most important thing a soldier could do. The war in France had ground to a virtual halt and now the armies of Britain, France and Germany lived in deep trenches and faced each other across the narrow strip of No man's land that ran nearly five hundred miles from Switzerland to the North Sea.

'I didn't join the army to dig holes in the ground,' growled Frank Mitchell. 'I joined to fight the bloody Germans.'

Ellis sighed and threw another shovel of earth onto the newly created parapet. What made the job so soul-destroying was knowing that once they had finished, they would undoubtedly be told to fill it in again. 'Digging trenches might just save your life one day, Frank,' he said. 'And anyway, you aren't digging. We are.'

Frank sniffed his disdain and settled himself onto the fire step. Casually he lit a cigarette, flicking the match onto the trench floor. 'You dig, I supervise,' he smiled, pointing to the single stripe on his arm. 'Perks of the rank.'

Lieutenant Newman, the officer recently assigned to their platoon, appeared around the corner of the trench. He was very young, barely out of public school, and was nervously fingering the wispy moustache he was still struggling to grow. 'How's it going, Corporal?' he asked.

'All fine, sir,' said Frank, straightening to attention. 'The trench is almost finished.'

'Yes,' said Newman, 'that's the problem. The Colonel says it's not deep enough. You've got to go down another two feet. See to it, Corporal.' He turned and strode away.

'Damn you, Frank,' stormed Bert Phillips. 'If you'd listened to instructions in the first place, we'd have been finished by now.'

Frank glared at him and snarled. 'You heard the man, start digging!'

*

One day the platoon was marched to nearby Southport and spent hours charging along the sand and up into the dunes. By late afternoon, however, everyone had had enough. The officers and NCOs had lost interest and the bored, exhausted soldiers were gathered together on the sea front.

'One hour,' called Sergeant Jenkins. 'One hour, that's what you've got. Go and find yourselves a cup of tea – or even a candyfloss, if that's what takes your fancy. But be back here by 17.00 or I'll have your guts for garters.'

*

Ellis and Danny headed into town, glad to be free of the army, even if not for long. At the far end of the main shopping street they paused and Ellis pointed. 'Look,' he said.

A dozen soldiers, dressed in the blue jackets that wounded men always wore, were making their way carefully across the road. Each of them had a bandage around his eyes and held firmly onto the shoulder of the man in front.

'Gas victims,' whispered Ellis, 'from the Front.'

For the first time the harsh reality of war was brought home to Danny. During all their training they had been constantly fed the one thought – that the British army was stronger and better than the Germans. But if the Germans were such poor fighters, why was the war lasting so long? The newspapers talked of victory and of ground gained but only a cursory glance at the casualty lists showed that if it was a victory it was one that was being gained at a terrible cost.

Ellis and Danny stood watching until the wounded men passed on, across the road and down a side alley.

'I hope I never get a wound like that,' said Ellis. 'I can't imagine never being able to see the hills again.' He shook his head. 'No, a quick bullet and then oblivion, that's much the better way.'

*

As the cold winds of February and early March set in, the unit became due for leave.

'Forty-eight hours, that's all you lot are worth,' Sergeant Jenkins informed them. 'Officers have two weeks, of course. You 'orrible lot – two days. And think yourselves lucky to get that.'

When Danny's turn came, he knew it would be impossible to travel home to Treorchy in the time he had available. He longed to see Angharad again but realised he would have to wait a while longer.

'Then you can come home with me,' Ellis said. 'We won't be there for long but if we can get away fast, as soon as we come off duty, and travel all night we should make it. My people will make you very welcome.'

As soon as they finished work for the day, Ellis and Danny set out for the station. On the crowded train to Caernarfon, Ellis was preoccupied. He was working on a new poem, he said. Several times he paused and asked Danny to listen.

'It sounds wonderful to me,' Danny said, 'but it is in Welsh and I can hardly understand a word you're on about.'

'I know,' Ellis smiled. 'I just need to read it aloud. It's as much about me reading as it is about you understanding. I'll try to translate but it won't be exact. Listen –

> We have no right to the stars
> Nor the homesick moon,
> Nor the clouds edged with gold
> In the centre of the long blueness.'

He shrugged. 'It's not the same in English. It loses something.'

Danny didn't know if the poem lost or gained. It sounded good to him.

It was late when they arrived at Caernarfon. They walked out of the station and managed to find a lift with a carter who was taking a stack of wood to Porthmadog. From there on, it was a case of slogging across the hills, talking about everything and anything to keep themselves going.

'Do you have a sweetheart?' Danny suddenly asked as they got closer to Ellis's home.

Ellis stopped for a moment. 'Yes,' he nodded. 'But we've agreed to go slowly for a while. When I get back, after the war, we'll pick it up again.'

They walked on and Danny thought, sadly, about Angharad. He could no more have distanced himself from her than he could have flown off the top of Cader Idris. She was a part of his soul, he decided, war or no war. He admired Ellis for his stance but he felt sorry and sad for him as well.

Dawn had broken by the time they reached the village of Trawsfynydd. They trudged on to the farm at Yr Ysgwrn. Danny was exhausted but Ellis was quietly excited. He was coming home. His mother answered his knock and a torrent of rapid Welsh flew from her lips as she held him tight.

'*Rhaid siarad Saesneg, Mam.* You'll have to speak in English,' Ellis said, pulling away from her. 'Danny has no Welsh.'

His mother wiped her hands on her pinafore. '*Croeso,*

Danny. Welcome.' She stood aside and ushered him across the hearth then busied herself with breakfast.

They sat in front of a huge log fire and were served plates heaped with ham and eggs. They drank scalding hot tea and then sat back, half asleep and dozing in the early morning light. Danny filled and lit the pipe he had recently bought while Ellis stared into the flames and stroked the head of his favourite Border collie. He whispered quietly to the dog, and Danny could have sworn the animal knew every word he was saying.

'How long do you have, boy?' asked Mrs Evans.

'We have to be back in camp tomorrow night.'

The woman nodded and began to clear away the dishes. She spoke in Welsh to her son and Ellis explained that Bob, his brother, would take them to Caernarfon in the dog cart in the morning. That would make the journey a little easier.

Danny smiled his thanks, lay back in his chair and closed his eyes. The room was warm and comforting and he felt wonderfully relaxed. He was asleep in minutes.

When he woke four hours later, Ellis had gone. The fire was still roaring and he knew that, if he did not want to waste the day, he had better move now. He climbed to his feet and stretched his arms. Mrs Evans came in from the kitchen, alerted by the noise of his boots on the flagstones.

'There is Ellis.' She motioned him to the window. A long ridge overlooked the house and he picked out Ellis's tall figure standing at the top of the slope.

'I expect he's writing poetry,' Danny said. 'In his head. He's going to win the Chair at the National Eisteddfod,' he gushed. 'He's read me his work. It's wonderful.'

Mrs Evans just smiled.

'I'd better join him, hadn't I?' said Danny. 'I expect he wants to show me around.'

*

The climb up the hill was short but steep.

'Come on, soldier boy,' Ellis called from the top of the slope. 'We've got a lot of walking to do.'

They spent the afternoon striding across the hills and fields, talking about anything but war. Dusk found them back at the farmhouse where dinner and Ellis's family were waiting. That evening Danny met his friend's father and brothers, now back home after a day spent working on the farm. There were eleven children in all and the names and faces swung past him like half-glimpsed shadows so that, later, he would have no real recall of what they looked or sounded like.

Late into the night they sat before the fire and talked. The men in the family soon went off to their beds – they would be up and away early the following day. But Ellis and his mother and Danny stayed as long as they could.

Danny talked about Angharad and his plans for the future. 'I want to work in the open air,' he declared. 'I hate the mine, being underground all day, the darkness, the dust and the noise – do you know, sometimes you can hear the earth creaking above your head. And sometimes more than that . . .' He reached down to stroke the ears of Ellis's dog. 'A farm, that's what I'd like, a little one. Not too big, just large enough for Angharad and me to manage. That's my dream, that's what I want when the war is over.' He fell silent.

Nobody moved, nobody spoke. A log rolled over and fell in the fireplace but still no one moved.

Chapter Five

Spring came late that year. The wind and rain hammered in off the Irish Sea and there were times when the men wondered if they would ever be warm again. They stood guard and went on interminable marches along the coast, always knowing that sooner or later they would be in France, fighting on the Western Front.

They were sitting, one night, in their hut, army greatcoats wrapped around them for warmth, bemoaning their situation. There was enough coal to light only one stove and that gave out just the faintest hint of heat. Frank Mitchell seemed to be hogging most of that, sitting with his legs akimbo and his backside perched against the top of the iron framework.

'What a life!' sighed Bert Phillips. 'I never knew I could be so cold. I feel like a bloody Eskimo.'

The hut door smashed open and Sergeant Jenkins stepped inside. 'What's that? Moaning about these lovely conditions?' He glared at Bert. 'When you get to France, my lad, you won't have a nice tin hut like this to keep you warm. You'll be sleeping in holes in the ground. You'll be thankful for one piece of tin, never mind a whole bleedin' hut of the stuff!'

Bert hung his head. 'Yes, Sarge,' he muttered.

Jenkins turned to fix Frank with a steely stare. 'Route march tomorrow, Corporal – all men to be fell in by 07.00. Make sure they're carrying full packs.' He turned to leave, and then paused, with the door wide open and the wind howling into the hut. What little warmth there was died instantly. 'I'd have thought intelligent soldiers like you would have used a bit of initiative – that's if you really do want to get warm.'

'How's that, Sergeant?' asked Frank.

Jenkins stared at him and shook his head in despair. 'God preserve me. Use your initiative, you 'orrible little soldier. You need fuel, things to burn if you want to keep warm.' Then he was gone, the door swinging wildly behind him in the wind.

Bert crossed the floor, reached out for the door and pulled it shut. 'Come on then, Frank,' he said. 'Let's see some action. You've got the stripe – what are we going to do?'

Frank stared at him blankly. 'I don't know. What can we do?'

'What we can do is find something to burn – you heard the man.'

Danny was on his feet. 'Like what?'

'Like the wood and coke at the back of the officers' quarters. They've got tons of the stuff over there. They'd never miss a few bucket loads.'

There was a general murmur of approval. 'Suits me,' said Tudor. 'Equal distribution of wealth, I always say.'

'Wait a minute.' Frank had moved away from his

position by the stove and now stood defiantly, blocking the hut door. 'Nobody is raiding the officers' coke supply. That's an offence, against all military regulations. If any of you go over there, I'll report you and you'll find yourselves on a charge quicker than you can blink.'

A tense hush fell across the room. Nobody doubted that Frank would carry out his threat and, instinctively, all eyes turned towards Ellis. Slowly, deliberately, he drew himself up to his full height and smiled at Frank. Frank tried to hold his gaze but failed dismally. He lowered his eyes, unsure what to do. He had the power of rank but that was all. And if it came to a fight, Frank was in no doubt who would win. He was no hero; he knew when he was beaten. 'Suit yourselves,' he shrugged. 'I don't care – as long as you don't get caught.'

He turned away, sulkily. Before he had even resumed his position by the stove, five of the platoon had stolen out of the door, armed with large metal buckets. It was a matter of only moments to cover the hundred yards to the officers' quarters.

'See what they're doing inside,' Ellis whispered to Danny. 'Then keep watch.'

Danny tiptoed to the window. Inside the hut three officers were gathered around an open fire, jackets off and braces hanging around their waists. All three had glasses of whisky in their hands. 'How the other half lives,' Danny whispered to himself. He signalled all clear and flattened himself against the side of the hut, watching through a gap in the curtains for any sign of movement.

The officers weren't going anywhere on such a bitter night. Once the door swung open but it was on the other side of the building and did not present a threat. A fourth officer, Lieutenant Newman from their platoon, entered the room, threw off his coat and Sam Browne belt and joined the others by the fire.

'All done,' said a sudden voice by Danny's ear. He swore he jumped six feet in the air but it was only Ellis. Together they made their way back to their hut.

'Piece of cake,' laughed Bert Phillips, ladling coal and kindling into one of the pot-bellied stoves. 'Now let's see about getting some heat into this place.'

Within a few minutes the room was luxuriously warm and the members of the platoon sat back, happily, on their bunks.

'You're a bloody marvel,' Tudor told Ellis. 'You should be wearing the corporal's stripes, not that useless donkey over there.'

Ellis glanced up from the poem he was working on and shrugged.

Only Danny saw the hatred in Frank Mitchell's eyes. And at that moment he knew there was going to be trouble.

*

At the beginning of April, Ellis was given six weeks' leave to go home and help with the ploughing on his family farm, a gift the Government granted most farmers' sons during the important planting season. Danny missed his friend and counted the days until his return. Friendship with Bert, Tudor and even Tommy Twice was one thing – it could not begin to compare with the comradeship he had forged with the poet-shepherd. Frank Mitchell, of course, could not resist the occasional dig.

'Lost your little friend, have you?' he sneered one night. 'What a shame, got nobody to hold your hand any more.' He kept his distance, however. He knew that Ellis would be back and, besides, Danny had friends now, people like Bert and Tudor. And Frank knew better than to tangle with any of them.

It was a long six weeks but at last the day came when Ellis finally arrived back in Litherland. 'I'm almost glad to be back,' he said. 'I'd forgotten how hard it is to walk behind a plough for ten hours a day.'

'You're getting soft, soldier boy,' Frank sneered. 'We've got a twenty-mile route march tomorrow. That should get you back in training.'

Ellis smiled but did not respond. Danny knew that, no matter what he said, his friend's mind was on the green hills and the lakes of Trawsfynydd.

*

They received their orders for service overseas at the beginning of June. The news was met with a combination of excitement and apprehension. The same thought was in everybody's mind – they had had their training; now would they be good enough? When the whole unit was awarded two weeks' embarkation leave, a manic gaiety filled the tin huts and barrack blocks.

'You know what this means?' said Danny. 'Next week I'll be seeing Angharad again. It seems so long. I can hardly remember what she looks like.'

Ellis slapped him on the back. 'Go on with you.'

Danny was sheepish. 'Look, I don't know what you think about this but . . .' He stopped, for some reason quite unable to go on.

Ellis sat alongside him. 'Come on, tell me.'

Danny breathed heavily through his mouth and began again in a rush. 'I'm seventeen now. I've trained with you all. I'm ready to fight with you. I think I'm a man – at least I feel like a man.'

'Danny, what are you trying to say?'

Danny bit his lip, his voice hoarse and trembling. 'I've asked Angharad to marry me. I've written to her and to my mam and the minister at my chapel. If they all agree, we're going to be married the week after next, before I go out to France.'

Ellis beamed with pleasure. 'Good for you, boy. I suppose there's no question that Angharad will say yes and I imagine the minister will do as he's asked, but what about your mother?'

'Oh she won't object. Not if it makes me happy.'

Ellis nodded. He stared, almost mournfully, at the floor of the hut. It did not take much to realise he was thinking about his own girl and the way he had put his life on hold.

Danny, however, had not finished. 'I know it's a lot to ask – it's such a long way, Trawsfynydd to Treorchy – but would you come . . .'

He saw Ellis hesitating and stopped, suddenly. 'If you don't want to . . .' he stuttered.

'It's not that. I'd be proud to come to your wedding. Not even Sergeant Jenkins could keep me away. I was just thinking whether I might deliver my Eisteddfod entry in person instead of trusting it to the post.'

Danny could have wept with joy. He went off for his leave train with Ellis's words ringing in his ears – if the wedding was on, a postcard to Trawsfynydd would bring him south quicker than a flock of summer sparrows.

*

As the train pulled into Treorchy Station, Danny saw Angharad almost immediately. She was standing at the back of the platform, close to the waiting-room door, her eyes eagerly scanning the carriages as they swept past. Then she saw him and waved. 'Danny,' she called. 'Danny!'

He had forgotten how beautiful she was. All the way home he had been dreaming of this moment, and now he found that he was shaking with excitement. He grabbed his pack and almost fell out of the carriage. The next moment she was in his arms, laughing and crying at the same time. 'Danny,' she whispered. 'Danny, it's been so long.'

They clung to each other until the platform emptied.

'Did you get my letter?' Danny gasped, at last.

Angharad nodded. She pulled away to arm's length and stared at him. 'Danny, you seem so different, so tall, so sure of yourself. You – you've grown up.'

He held onto her hands and spoke again, directly into her face. 'But did you read my letter?'

'Yes,' she said. 'And if this is by way of a second proposal, the answer's the same. Yes.'

He caught her by the waist and swung her around, shouting and laughing at the top of his voice. 'I love you, Annie, more than anything in the world. I can't believe it – we're going to be married.'

'Stop, Danny,' Angharad said. 'Stop it. I'll be under the train in a minute.'

He put her down, gently. 'We're going to be married,' he whispered.

*

The next few days passed in a whirl of activity. Danny sent off his postcard to Trawsfynydd and waited for Ellis's reply. It arrived by return post. He was coming.

Danny travelled down to Cardiff to escort Ellis back to Treorchy. They met on the crowded platform of the Great Western Railway station and shook hands solemnly.

'As befits a man about to take on the duties and responsibilities of married life,' said Ellis. 'Now show me the famous Rhondda valley.'

The journey to Treorchy was long and slow, the train stopping at every tiny station and halt. Danny pointed out the pits and gave names to all the small communities while Ellis gazed on in incredulity.

'How can so many people live together in one area?' he said. 'How do they cope? There's no room to breathe.'

'I thought you'd lived down here for a few months?' said Danny.

'I did. But I don't remember it like this. Perhaps I was just younger, more accepting.'

They lapsed into silence, until Danny remembered. He leaned forward and tapped his friend on the knee. 'Did you send off your entry for the Eisteddfod?'

Ellis shook his head. 'No, I've had a change of heart. I threw away that poem and started a new one. It'll take me a while to finish it. It's long, 500 lines, called *"Yr Arwr"* – it means "The Hero". You know the story of Prometheus?'

Danny shrugged. 'Never heard of him. Or is it her?'

'Him. He was the Greek who stole fire and gave it to mankind.'

As far as Danny was concerned, Ellis could have been talking in Greek, not just talking about it. But, content in his friend's company, he let him ramble on.

*

The wedding took place the following day, a simple affair in the chapel that Danny and Angharad had attended since they were babies. Afterwards they moved to the chapel vestry where her family had prepared food. There were only a few people present, mostly family and a few close friends. Danny's mother sat quietly in the corner and did not speak. Her sadness seemed to have grown since Danny had been away.

Ellis stood at the front of the hall with Danny and his new wife. He had only a few short hours before starting back for north Wales. 'It's been so good to meet you, Angharad,' he said. 'You'll never know how much you've become a part of my life over the past months.'

Angharad leaned forward and kissed him, lightly, on the cheek. 'But you're part of my life, too. Ever since Danny first wrote to me and spoke about you. You will try to keep him safe when you finally get out to . . . to . . .' Emotion welled up in her chest, stopping her words.

Ellis understood and, softly, laid his hand on her arm. 'I'll do my best, Angharad, I promise you that. Now, I've got a present for you. It's nothing much but I hope you'll like it.' Awkwardly, he reached into his jacket pocket and passed across an envelope. Inside was a single sheet of paper.

Angharad pulled it out and read it, slowly.

'I don't usually write in English,' Ellis said, 'so if it seems a little clumsy, forgive me. But the words are from the heart.'

Angharad's eyes were wet as she passed the sheet back to Ellis.

'You read it to me. Please?'

56

Ellis began to read, slowly, haltingly, his voice full of emotion. When he finished, for a few moments there was silence. 'It's not for publication, mind,' he said. 'That's for you – and only you.' He smiled weakly. 'Perhaps when I'm old and famous you can bring it out and sell it.'

'I'll treasure it for ever, Ellis,' said Angharad. 'God bless you and keep you safe.'

Ellis looked down quickly. For the first time Danny realised that his friend was not immortal. And neither was he. For the first time he understood the terror of what they would soon be facing.

Chapter Six

They left Liverpool by train, dozens of men crushed together into carriages and wagons. Ellis managed to find an empty compartment and kept guard at the door while Danny and the others threw themselves and their equipment inside.

'Snug as a bug in a rug,' quipped Bert, throwing his rifle and pack onto the luggage rack and settling himself onto one of the seats.

'Cushions, too,' said Tudor. 'We do travel first class in the Royal Welch Fusiliers.'

'Officer coming,' hissed Tommy Twice from his position by the door.

There was a flurry of activity from the corridor and then Lieutenant Newman pushed open the door and peered into the compartment. 'All right in here?'

'All fine, sir, thank you,' Bert replied.

Newman stroked his blond moustache and nodded. 'Good, good. Well, it's going to be a long journey so settle down and do your best.'

He passed on up the corridor, Sergeant Jenkins following faithfully in his wake. At the end of the carriage the Sergeant paused and threw a withering glance over his shoulder. 'Enjoy the comfort while you can. However crowded this train is, you can bet your lives it's a lot better than what's waiting for you on the other side of the Channel.'

Bert Phillips stared after him. 'He's a right Job's comforter, ain't he? What do you think he meant by that?'

'I'm sure we'll find out shortly,' said Danny. He settled back in his seat and pulled out Angharad's most recent letter. She must have written it the day he left Treorchy.

> 'My dearest Danny,' she wrote. 'The town is empty and sad now that you have gone again. Tonight I will climb up the hill – our hill – and sit there for a while, thinking of you. Please, for me, do not take any silly risks. I know you will do your duty but remember you also have a duty to me now. I know I am being selfish but I can't help it.
>
> Keep yourself safe, Danny, and come home soon.
>
> All my love, Angharad.
>
> P.S. Give Ellis my love, too.'

Danny folded the letter and put it into his breast pocket. He smiled to himself and felt a deep warmth flooding through his body.

'Look at him,' said Tudor. 'Like the cat that got the bleedin' cream.'

Everyone laughed, and Danny laughed along with them. 'Angharad sends her love,' he told Ellis.

The tall shepherd nodded. 'Thank her for me when you write,' he said and sat back on the cushions, studying the pictures and prints on the compartment wall behind Danny's head. Relics of a more peaceful age, advertisements for holidays in places like Morecambe, Blackpool and Rhyl, they seemed out of place in a train full of soldiers armed with rifles and bayonets. He pointed to one of the prints, a garishly-coloured picture of Dover Castle and the town's pier. 'Look at that – "Come to the South Coast for the Day". It strikes me we'll be having a bit more than just a day out when we finally get to Dover.'

Nobody spoke but Ellis's words seemed to sum up what all of them were feeling. Danny closed his eyes and tried to think of Angharad. What would she be doing now? he wondered. Somehow her image would not come and he drifted off to sleep.

The journey took them all day. Several times their train was shunted into a siding to allow faster express trains to shoot past.

'Probably some general off to lunch at the Savoy,' said Bert as yet another train hammered past in a flurry of smoke and soot. He threw open the window and stuck out his head. 'Hey, you lot, don't you know we're the Royal Welch Fusiliers? We're on the way to win your bleedin' war for you!'

When they finally reached the port of Dover, it was already dark. They had had no food all day, just an issue of water. Bert and Tudor were soon complaining loudly.

'There'll be food when we get on the boat,' Sergeant Jenkins told them. 'Until then you'll have to shut up and suffer like the rest of us.'

The train was standing in a marshalling yard at the western end of the docks. Huge arc lights illuminated the perimeter of the base, making the place as bright as day. There they waited – and kept on waiting.

'There's been a delay,' Sergeant Jenkins told them. 'Submarines in the Channel. We could be here for hours yet.'

'He doesn't have to sound so happy about it,' moaned Tudor.

'Can we get out and stretch our legs, Sarge?' asked Bert.

Jenkins rounded on him. 'No you cannot! If I see anyone out of this train they'll be on a charge quicker than they can remember their own name. Sit still and think of the King.' He moved on up the corridor.

'Think of the King?' sighed Bert. 'I bet he isn't hot and bored like us.'

'Or hungry,' said Danny.

Ellis was staring at the perimeter fence. It lay just fifty yards away and beyond the tall strands of wire stood a row of houses. In the middle of the row, surrounded by clouds of billowing steam, was a fish shop. Customers came and went and they could smell the aroma of the shop – and its produce – sharp, succulent and inviting on the breeze.

'It's bad enough being hungry,' said Tudor, 'but parking us opposite that place is sheer cruelty. Wait till I get my hands on the blighter who put us here.'

'If it wasn't for them lights,' Bert ventured, 'I reckon one of us, a little one, could get under that fence. Look, you can see where the wire is stretched and broken. There, by that stanchion. It's probably where the dock workers get out for their chips of an evening.'

Danny followed his outstretched arm. He was right; there was a definite break in the wire. 'It's no use to us, though,' he said, 'not in this light. Sergeant Jenkins would spot anything moving out there. We'd stand out like fleas on a clean sheet.'

As he spoke there came a sudden high-pitched wailing from the dock behind them, a loud and piercing siren that cut through the night like an explosion. One by one the arc lights went out. Inside two minutes they were sitting in pitch darkness.

'It's a zeppelin raid,' said Bert. 'This is our chance. Quick, pool your money.' He threw his hat onto the seat. Within seconds it was full of loose change. 'Come on, Danny.'

He unlocked the door and dropped onto the shingle of the siding. Danny followed him, expecting at any moment to hear the Sergeant's strident bellow echoing down the side of the carriages. Nothing happened. Keeping low, they raced for the fence. As they thought, there was a gap, low down but big enough to allow a small man through. 'It'll have to be you,' said Bert. 'You're the only one small enough to fit through there. I'll hold up the wire and keep watch. Buy what you can but do it quickly.'

He bent and, straining every muscle in his body, pulled up the heavy wire. Danny slipped underneath, sprang to his feet and sped across the road. It was a matter of only minutes to relieve the shop owner of half his stock of fish and chips. Soon he was back at the wire.

'All right?' asked Bert.

Danny nodded and pushed his precious packages through the gap. Then he threw himself down onto his back and began to squirm through after them.

'Well, well, well,' said a familiar voice. 'What do we have here?'

Danny looked up into the steel-hard eyes of Sergeant Jenkins.

The NCO's hands were clasped behind his back; his foot was tapping dangerously. 'Privates Jones and Phillips, of all people. If anyone was going to do it I just knew it would be you.'

The packages of fish and chips lay accusingly on the ground. For what seemed like hours, nobody moved.

'What did I tell you lot?' asked Jenkins.

'Not to get out of the train, Sarge,' said Danny.

Sergeant Jenkins nodded and there was a long silence. Suddenly, eyes twinkling, he reached down and picked up one of the smaller packages. He weighed it in his hand like a grenade. 'How kind of you, Private Jones – fish and chips for my supper. I was beginning to feel a little peckish.'

He jerked his head towards the waiting train. 'On yer way, quick. I ain't seen nothing.'

They gathered up their parcels and scampered back to the carriage. Eager hands helped them inside. Behind them, Sergeant Jenkins smiled grimly – they were becoming real soldiers at last.

*

They finally embarked on the cross-channel steamer at three in the morning. As the troops climbed wearily up the gangplank, Sergeant Jenkins and the other NCOs stood at the bottom handing out steel helmets.

'Helmets, troops, for the use of,' laughed Jenkins. 'One for each man.'

'My life is haunted by bloody tin,' moaned Bert. 'Tin huts and now tin flamin' helmets.'

Sergeant Jenkins glared at him. 'Not tin, you 'orrible little man. Steel!' He rapped his fist on the helmet, the blow seeming to force Bert's head down into his shoulder blades.

'Best British steel! This helmet will save your life, boy. The first time a lump of shrapnel lands on your noddle, you'll be grateful for it, right enough.'

As it turned out, Bert soon found another, more immediate, use for the helmet.

'Sergeant, Bert Phillips is being seasick,' called Tommy Twice.

'Seasick? How can he be seasick? We haven't even left port yet.' Jenkins crossed to the rail and found Bert throwing up, violently, into his new steel helmet.

'Sorry, Sarge,' he groaned. 'We don't have sea at Birmingham. Sorry.'

Jenkins grinned, maliciously. 'Sorry? You will be, Private Phillips. That helmet is government property and you're misusing it. Defaulters Parade tomorrow – you're on a charge, laddie.'

Danny found a sheltered spot on the starboard side of the ship and he and Ellis quickly settled down for what was left of the night. Amazingly, despite the chill wind and a growing sense of excitement, they were both asleep in moments.

When he awoke, Danny's first sight was of a slate-grey sea rolling in great slabs towards him. On the horizon lay a long line of low cliffs. 'France!' he whispered.

Boulogne harbour was full of ships, transports and naval vessels alike. Outside the breakwater, low, sleek destroyers patrolled the waterways, on the look-out for German U-boats, and it took them over an hour to inch their way in through the anti-submarine nets that had been laid across the mouth of the harbour.

With the coming of war, Boulogne had clearly become a military town. There were red-capped policemen on every corner while groups of soldiers stood clustered around the doors and tables of all the wine shops. Wagons and limbers of the Royal Horse Artillery kept galloping through the narrow streets while despatch riders on their motorbikes roared along the thoroughfares in clouds of choking dust. Here and there, wounded men in their distinctive blue jackets limped unsteadily along the pavements.

'Anyone would think there was a war on,' said Tudor.

It took some time to disembark but at last they were drawn up alongside yet another set of railway tracks. Bert, rapidly recovered now that he was again on dry land, nudged Ellis and pointed at the trucks that awaited them. 'I see what Sergeant Jenkins meant. Those aren't railway carriages; they're cattle trucks. Look at that.'

A stencilled motto stood out starkly on the side of the nearest wagon – '*Hommes 40, Chevaux 8*'.

'Nice to know the horses get more space than soldiers,' said Ellis as they filed towards the truck door and clambered inside.

Straw had been spread across the floor. It looked old and dirty but the men were so worn out that most of them simply threw themselves down and closed their eyes. It wasn't long before they were all scratching and complaining.

'Learning to cope with fleas and lice is part of a soldier's life,' said Sergeant Jenkins. 'This is where your real training begins.'

They waited for several hours before the train finally trundled off. It was another long journey. For two days they lay in their cattle wagon as the engine struggled to make ten miles an hour. First they headed south, then circled around to the north again before finally turning eastwards.

'I don't know if this is meant to deceive the Germans,' quipped Bert, 'but it's confusing the hell out of me.'

'I reckon,' said Tudor, 'that they've got us over here and now they don't know what to do with us. We'll probably stay on this damned train for the rest of the war.'

They played cards and sang the usual soldiers' songs in an attempt to keep their spirits up. The boredom was only broken by occasional stops when the doors were thrown open and they were allowed out for exercise. Food was provided by the battalion cooks, basic but filling, served from huge dixies that had been set up along the side of the tracks.

And as they journeyed eastwards, they became aware of a distant grumbling over the horizon. It grew and swelled, rising to a crescendo before dying away. Then the whole sequence started again.

'What is it?' asked Tudor. 'A thunderstorm?'

'Bloody strange thunderstorm,' shrugged Bert.

It was past midnight on the second day and the train was stopped in a siding, miles out in the country. The wagon doors had been thrown open to allow fresh air inside. In the distance the sky flickered with flashes of lightning. 'Not thunder,' said Sergeant Jenkins, appearing quietly in the doorway. His usual sarcasm was gone. 'That's guns. Our guns. And that's the way we're heading.'

Ellis glanced at Danny and tried to smile. 'We have unleashed the dogs of war, haven't we?' he said softly.

'Pardon?'

'Shakespeare. It's from Julius Caesar – "Cry havoc and unleash the dogs of war".'

Sergeant Jenkins stood, breathing lightly, alongside him. He stared at Ellis and then at all the men in his charge. They were lying or sitting hunched across the floor of the truck, eyes wide with wonder. All of them were staring at the sky to the east. Like steel to a magnet, their eyes were drawn to the lights. 'Personally, I prefer the Bible, Private Evans.'

'Sarge?'

Jenkins shrugged. 'The Book of Isaiah, Chapter 13, I think, though I could be wrong. After all I ain't a well-read man like you – "We have made a covenant with death and with hell we are at agreement." Here, you can make use of this, I'm sure.'

He pushed a bottle of French brandy into Ellis's hands.

'He doesn't drink!' called Tudor. 'It's wasted on him.'

Ellis passed the bottle to Bert and watched as he raised it, gratefully, to his lips. The Sergeant drifted away and the men were left to stare at the lights on the horizon and to listen to the roar of the deadly guns.

'For what we are about to receive,' said Tudor, 'may the Lord make us truly thankful.'

Chapter Seven

Danny ducked his head under the remains of an old foundation wall and followed the man in front across a sea of mud. Rain slanted down into his face, running off his waterproof cape and down the neck of his khaki tunic. His puttees were soaked and already his feet felt wet and cold.

'Oh my, I don't want to die, I want to go home,' sang somebody from the ranks behind him.

Danny thought he recognised Bert's voice but then came the harsh bark of an NCO and silence descended across the line of walking men.

Acclimatisation, Lieutenant Newman had called it. All of them were to spend short periods in the front line, supporting other more experienced units. They had been attached to the 15th Battalion of the Fusiliers and two groups of men had already gone up to the trenches. They had come back muddy, dishevelled and with an air of horror about them that separated them from those who had not yet had the experience.

'We meet our guide at 20.00 hours,' Lieutenant Newman told them. 'That means we leave here three hours earlier, at 17.00. Sergeant Jenkins will give you your individual assignments.'

And so they had set off. The first few miles were easy enough, apart from the rain that had seemed to start as soon as they formed up. When they rendezvoused with their guide, a young lieutenant from the Sherwood Foresters, the war seemed to come suddenly closer. The soldier was dressed in a sheepskin coat, hacked off by a bayonet or blunt knife just below the waist, and carried a short-magazine Lee Enfield rifle. The man was caked in mud and there was little to distinguish him as an officer. He stared at the newcomers with ill-concealed contempt.

'Keep your men quiet,' he told Newman. 'Jerry – Fritz, call him what you like – is out tonight, mending his wire. If he twigs that reinforcements are coming up – even useless ones like you – he'll put a strafe across. And you wouldn't like that, believe me.'

He turned abruptly away and led off across a muddy field, the long line of nervous men following in his wake. From ahead came the occasional flash of a star shell and then, from somewhere further south, the regular and insistent rat-a-tat-tat of machine-gun fire.

'Not the most reassuring of sounds,' whispered Ellis.

Danny did not reply. His mouth was suddenly dry and he was finding it hard to swallow.

At the edge of the field they entered a shallow trench. It ran for half a mile, sometimes winding its way around shattered buildings, sometimes forcing its way out into the open. The open stretches made Danny feel very vulnerable. He could see mounds of grass and mud and a few limbless trees. He knew that if he could see them, so

70

too could the Germans. They passed through several more communication trenches, trying hard not to slip off the duckboards that lined the floor, and fall into the mud that lay, several feet thick, beneath.

'Quiet now,' whispered the guide. 'The front line is two hundred yards that way.' He pointed down the trench. 'I'm going back to pick up another party. Report to the officer at the other end of this trench.' He paused to speak to Lieutenant Newman. 'You'll be OK,' he said and, without another word, disappeared into the darkness.

Newman swallowed hard and, followed by Sergeant Jenkins, began to make his way down the trench. After a few hundred yards they passed a large dugout, like a cave, cut from the side of the trench wall. Inside, a group of men squatted on planks of wood, gazing silently at the light of a single candle in the centre. The flame flickered in the wind and the men's faces were gaunt and tired. It could have been a scene from hell. The men had eyes only for the candle and did not look up as the newcomers trudged silently past.

'Dear God,' breathed Frank Mitchell. 'What have we come to?'

Danny glanced at the Corporal's hollow, ashen face. He was obviously as scared as the rest of them. The trouble was, he showed it.

Eventually they emerged into a deep trench zigzagging at right angles across their front. Fire steps lined the trench and every twenty or so yards, a deeper shade of darkness showed where an indenture or firing-bay had been cut into the front wall, reaching out into No man's land. Above their heads they could see huge coils of single-strand barbed wire.

'Wish I'd had the contract to supply barbed wire to the army,' said Bert. 'There must be a thousand miles of the stuff laid down between the lines.'

'So this is it,' said Ellis. 'We've finally reached the front line.'

A strange farmyard smell, combined with strong disinfectant, hung about the trench. It made Danny wrinkle his nose in disgust. And over it all lay a sweet odour like pear drops.

'Gas,' said Sergeant Jenkins.

'The smell of death,' Ellis whispered, his eyes wide.

Sergeant Jenkins shook his head. 'Less of the bloody poetics, thank you, Private Evans. Keep your respirators handy and get 'em on quick if the gas alarm goes off.'

He began to detail them off. Danny and Ellis found themselves pushed into a firing-bay in the front wall of the trench. It was already occupied by two soldiers, both young and both as hollow-eyed as the men they had passed in the dugout. They nodded a brief hello and then carried on with what they had been doing, one cooking a stew of some description on a small stove, the other taking brief glimpses over the parapet through a trench periscope.

'Jerry's out tonight,' the watcher said to no one in particular.

'So we've been told,' ventured Ellis.

The watcher carried on talking, as if Ellis had never opened his mouth. 'He's mending his wire, directly opposite. If you listen you can hear him.'

They craned their ears. The thump of wooden mallets on stakes and the occasional muttered oath carried clearly through the night air.

'Shouldn't we shoot at them or something?' Danny asked.

The soldier glared at him. 'Why? If we leave him alone, he'll leave us alone. He's not such a bad bloke, is Jerry. He doesn't want trouble and strife any more than we do. It's only the generals who want to win battles in this war. It'd be a grand life without them.'

He bent and peered again into the periscope. Then he beckoned Danny forward. 'Come and take a look.'

Danny put his eye to the glass. At first glance he could see nothing but darkness.

'Look to the left,' said the soldier. 'Focus on the tree.'

Danny swung the periscope around. The stump of a long-dead tree, battered and raked with bullet holes, loomed into focus. Beyond it lay craters and coils of rusting wire.

'That's No man's land, for you. Now look beyond our wire and you'll see Jerry.'

He was right. Barely a quarter of a mile away, huddled shapes were moving carefully about, carrying loads or swinging hammers in the darkness. It seemed so strange to finally see German soldiers in the flesh. Danny stood aside to let Ellis take a turn.

'The lines are quite close here,' said the periscope man. 'A few hundred yards, that's all. Sometimes we even talk to them – a couple of their men speak better English than I do.'

It was strange, the way these men spoke about the enemy soldiers. Back home it was all Hun or Boche, the baby-killers of Belgium. Here the Germans were called an almost affectionate Jerry or Fritz and getting on with a peaceful life seemed more important than hatred or killing.

'Don't get me wrong,' said the soldier, 'we'll shoot him or stick him with a bayonet when we have to – like he will us if he gets the chance. But that's in the heat of battle, as the papers love to call it. It just makes more sense to live in harmony as long as we can.' He paused, sniffed derisively and raised his eyebrows in mock alarm. 'Maybe we'll have a trench raid or two before you leave. You'll see plenty of action then.' He resumed his position at the periscope.

The other soldier suddenly looked up and spoke for the first time. 'You blokes got any food with you?'

Danny rummaged in his haversack and handed over a tin of meat.

The soldier pulled out his bayonet and expertly opened the tin. He sniffed at the contents. 'Not bad. Don't know what it is but it'll make this lot go a bit further.' He cut the meat into small chunks and dropped them carefully into the stew. Then he lapsed into morose silence once more. When the meal was ready, Danny ate heartily. He hadn't realised quite how hungry he was.

74

It was a cold, wet night. They settled down in what the periscope man called 'funk holes', small indentures cut into the side of the firing-bay and, covered by coats and capes, tried their best to sleep. It was difficult with the enemy being so close and Danny could not quite erase from his mind the image of a huge German, rifle and bayonet in hand, suddenly appearing on the parapet above him.

He supposed he must have slept because one minute it was dark, the next, light. Figures were beginning to move about in the trench outside the bay.

'Come on,' said the periscope man. 'Morning "Stand To".'

They picked up their rifles, adjusted the webbing that held their entrenching tools and bayonets, and stood waiting. Presently a pair of officers, one of them Lieutenant Newman, appeared in the entrance to the firing-bay. Neither of them spoke. They looked around, nodded approvingly and then moved on.

Sergeant Jenkins put his head through the opening. 'Survived your first night, then?' he asked. He glanced at their tired, strained faces and winked. 'You'll get used to it. I'll be back with your rum ration presently.'

The cook sniffed scornfully at his departing back. 'Don't listen to him. You might have to put up with it but you never get used to it.'

'Cheer up, Charlie,' said the other man. 'You heard the bloke – rum ration's coming soon. How about a bit of bacon for breakfast, eh?'

He and the cook set to, opening the tins of bacon they kept in their haversacks and then frying the stringy bits of meat.

Danny took the opportunity to have another look through the periscope. In daylight No man's land seemed very different. The craters, he noticed, were half-filled with water, and bits of old clothing and equipment lay scattered across the ground. Nothing moved and he could have been staring at the surface of the moon. Then his eye fell on what looked like a forgotten scarecrow attached to the wire in front of the bay. The scarecrow was dressed in a grey coat and there were wisps of yellow straw falling out from underneath his cap, across his forehead. With a start he realised that it was not a scarecrow – it was a man. He fell back with a gasp.

'Oh, just seen Herman, have you?' said the periscope man. 'He's been there since Jerry's last raid. Got himself caught on the wire and our machine guns did the rest. We've left him there – feels like he's part of the scenery now.'

Gently, he took the periscope from Danny's hands. 'Take a tip from me, mate, don't look too often. It doesn't do your mind any good, wondering what's happening over there.' He gestured with his arm. 'And besides, the more you use the periscope, the more likely Jerry is to see it. Before you know it, he'll have a sniper training his rifle on you. And that'll be the end of everything for you.'

Danny shuddered and sat on the fire step to eat his bacon. It was a long, trying day. Much of it they spent carrying food and ammunition from the communication trenches up to the front line. The occasional shell went over, one of them landing and exploding just fifty yards to their rear.

'Trench mortars,' said the cook. 'We call them minnies – the German name is *minenwerfer* or something like that. Don't worry: Jerry's aim is lousy. Look, if you've got good eyes, you can watch them wobbling through the air. That should give you some idea where they're going to land. You'll soon get to know the one that's coming your way.' He glanced around. 'He knows we're carrying up supplies. This is his way of letting us know he's still there.'

Staring around the trench, Danny could see that none of the old hands took much notice of the shells.

Frank Mitchell, however, heard the whine of their approach and shuddered and shrank into his collar every time. Once, when a shell burst close by, he was unable to stand it any longer. He hurled his load away and dived for the bottom of the trench, hands clasped behind his neck for protection. 'That was close,' he said, once the noise of the explosion had died away.

The cook and the periscope man stared at him as he climbed to his feet. His uniform was covered with mud and there was a wild stare in his eyes.

'Silly sod,' said the periscope man. 'You never hear the one that gets you.'

He turned to Ellis and Danny. 'I hope all your NCOs aren't like that. If they are, you boys haven't got a bloody snowball's chance in hell.'

*

It was past midnight when Danny was woken by shouts and crashes from the trench to his left. A short, sharp explosion told him that a hand grenade had been thrown.

'Trench raid,' said the periscope man. 'About fifty yards to our left. Stay here but get up on the fire step ready. They'll be retiring in a few minutes and we should be able to get in a few shots at their flank.'

Danny and Ellis climbed up on the step beside the others. Two more grenades were thrown, the explosions lighting up the night sky, then dying away.

'Won't be long now.'

Suddenly there were grey shapes up and running across their field of vision. The Germans were heading back to their own lines. A loud bang from beside his right ear told Danny that the periscope man had fired. 'Damn it. Missed the beggar!'

Danny took careful aim at one of the shapes and, as he had been taught on the range back in Wrexham, squeezed the trigger of his rifle. The figure crumpled and lay still.

'Keep firing,' said the cook, blazing away more in hope than expectation.

Finally, however, they heard a shout – 'Cease firing' – and they threw themselves down onto the earth inside the bay. I've just killed a man, Danny thought, snuffed out his life like I would a fly or a wasp. And then he began to shake. Ellis took hold of his arm.

'Don't worry about him,' said the periscope man. 'It often takes you like that, the first time you shoot somebody. He'll be all right – it was a bloody good shot.'

Danny sat and slowly the shaking stopped.

Ellis kept hold of his arm and spoke gently. 'Are you all right, Danny?'

Danny widened his eyes and inhaled deeply through his mouth. He nodded. 'I'm fine. It was just realising what I'd done.'

'I suppose that's why we're here,' said Ellis. 'It's our job. We may not like it but it's something we'll all have to do, sooner or later.'

Danny shrugged. 'I know. But I think I've just understood what an awful job it is. That man, the German I shot, he could have an Angharad waiting for him back home in Hamburg or wherever he lived. And now she'll never see him again.'

Ellis did not reply.

*

When they came out of the lines three days later, they all felt as if they had aged thirty years. Weary, aching with cold and fatigue, they marched back to their billets. They were veterans now; they had seen war and endured it. They had survived – at least for the time being.

Chapter Eight

That summer Ellis finished his entry for the National Eisteddfod.

'Come on then, Hedd Wyn,' Danny pleaded, 'let's hear it.' He sat back alongside Bert and Tudor, listening to the rolling cadences of Ellis's poem.

'It's all in bloody Welsh,' said Bert.

Danny nudged him with his elbow. 'Of course it is. He only writes in Welsh. They wouldn't want an English poem at the National Eisteddfod, would they?'

The Birmingham lad shook his head. 'Can't understand a bloomin' word.'

Because it was in Welsh, it took Ellis some time to convince Lieutenant Newman and the other officers that what he had written did not breach security. None of them read or spoke Welsh and for a while it seemed as if he might miss the deadline for entries. At last, however, everything was agreed and, with his pen name of Fleur-de-lis attached, the poem was sent off to the Eisteddfod committee.

'The winning entry?' Danny asked.

Ellis shrugged. 'I hope so. I've worked hard enough at it. I suppose this experience has to be useful for something.' He gestured at the shattered landscape. They were five or six miles behind the front, out on rest, but the area had been fought over, several times, and the ruined buildings simply reminded them that this was a country at war.

They had spent several more periods in the front line, growing more experienced all the time. Danny was surprised how quickly he grew hardened to the dirt and filth, the foul smells and the long, wakeful nights. Even the ever-present rats, grown bloated and huge on the corpses out in No man's land, became just part of the scenery. The one thing he never grew used to was the sound of birds high overhead. All day long larks soared and sang above them and several times small thrushes and sparrows landed briefly on the trench parapet.

'Listen,' said Ellis, one night. 'That's an owl.'

Danny listened carefully. Ellis was right; it was an owl perched on one of the shattered trees out in No man's land, calling mournfully into the darkness.

'You'd think this was the last place on earth to find birds,' Danny said, 'but I've heard more here, in the trenches, than I ever did back home.'

*

And then, on their third visit, when they were just beginning to think they had seen everything there was to see, the platoon suffered its first casualty. With hindsight Danny realised it was inevitable, sooner or later, but at the time it hit them all hard, much harder than any of them could have imagined.

Danny and Ellis were squatting in a makeshift dugout on the night before they were due for relief, trying hard to catch a few minutes' sleep. The night was still, with barely a breath of wind. Then, distantly but distinctly, they heard a muffled plop from the German lines.

'Minnie,' Danny announced casually.

Ellis clutched at his arm. 'This one's coming our way,' he said, urgently. 'Get down!'

There was a whirling sound as if a stick had been thrown through the air, and the mortar shell exploded in the trench outside. Danny felt the blast like a fist slamming into his chest. Helpless as a rag doll, he was picked up and flung against the back wall of the dugout. As he lay, trying to recover his breath, he heard an ominous shout from the trench and recognised Sergeant Jenkins's voice.

'Stretcher bearers, quickly!'

They poured out of the dugout, eager to see what had happened, and came face to face with the sergeant. He was covered with dark earth and his uniform was stained with something deeper, blacker. With a lurch of his stomach, Danny realised it was blood.

'Get back inside,' Jenkins said. 'You can't do anything to help.'

'Who is it, Sarge?' asked Bert.

Jenkins stared him in the eye. 'Private Thomas. What do you lot call him? Tommy Twice?'

'Is he . . .?'

'Yes, he's dead. Took the full blast. Now I won't tell

you again – get back into the dugout and stay out of the way.'

Around the corner of the trench, Danny could see a pair of legs lying in the mud, twisted and motionless. The top half of the body was already covered with a ground sheet. They filed back into the darkness of the dugout and sat around the walls, each of them lost in his own thoughts.

'Poor old Tommy Twice,' said Bert. And that was it, his epitaph.

*

They were relieved the next day and went back to their billets behind the lines. All the way, as they marched, Danny kept thinking of the small man who had been with them since the beginning. He hadn't asked for much, just a little friendship and to be part of the great adventure. And now he was gone, wiped out as quickly as a dream. It wasn't fair.

Sergeant Jenkins knew better than to let them brood on Tommy's death. Within hours of reaching their base, they were busy on route marches, practice assaults on heavily defended positions and supply details. For days on end they worked, and fell, exhausted, onto their blankets each night. Soon Tommy was only a memory and it was almost a relief to go back into the lines.

On their next visit to the front, Ellis and Danny were detailed to take part in a trench raid.

'Prisoners are what we need,' Sergeant Jenkins explained. 'The Brass Hats want to know who's in the lines opposite, what their strength is, that type of thing – nothing to worry your little heads. All you're concerned about is the prisoner. So it's in quick, grab one of the Jerries and then get out again.'

They were to be part of the support group, lying out in No man's land while the others went in to take the prisoner. Along with Bert and Frank Mitchell, they were to give covering fire to help the raiders withdraw.

'And mind you don't open fire until we get past you,' Jenkins said. 'I don't want any of you trigger-happy beggars shooting me in the backside.'

Bert grinned but a withering glance from the Sergeant made him quickly lower his head and find something important to study on the dugout floor.

They blackened their faces with burnt cork and waited. Danny felt the nerves tingling in his stomach but knew he was one of the lucky ones. He would have hated having to go into the German trench armed with Mills bombs and home-made coshes. Much better to be up out of the chaos, waiting for the raiders to come back.

Soon after midnight one of the corporals came around with the rum jar and the members of the raiding party were given an extra tot.

'Dutch courage?' Ellis said. He shook his head as the corporal slipped a tin mug into his hand but before the man could move on, Bert reached across to take the drink.

He happily downed Ellis's share, then winked and

smiled at him. 'Praise the Lord and pass the ammunition,' he said. 'Thank God for a teetotaller – every platoon should have one.'

Finally Sergeant Jenkins gave the word and the party slipped out of their trenches, climbing the wooden ladders that had been put in position. They crawled over the sandbags in front of the trenches and then inched their way between the coils of protecting wire. Moving slowly, on all fours, they made their way across No man's land, working around the bomb craters and trying to avoid the filthy water that lay thickly in every hollow.

'Support party, wait here,' whispered Sergeant Jenkins at last. 'Keep a careful watch for us.'

Danny settled down on the mud and eased his rifle to his shoulder. He was conscious of Ellis and Bert on his right. Frank lay several yards away on his left. They waited for what seemed like hours but there was no sound from the German trenches ahead of them. Danny could see the enemy wire but nothing moved and everything seemed unnaturally still and quiet.

'I reckon they've been captured,' said Frank suddenly. 'I say we should head back to our own lines.' His voice was loud in the still night, carrying clearly across No man's land.

'Shut up, you fool,' hissed Ellis. 'The Jerry trenches are only twenty yards away. If they'd been captured we'd have heard it. Jenkins is just waiting his moment.'

They fell silent. The waiting continued. Danny could imagine how Frank was feeling. Every second he expected to see a star shell burst overhead or feel a rifle bullet slam into his chest. Nothing happened.

'I can't stand this,' whispered Frank. 'I'm giving them another minute, and then I'm off.' As he spoke, the night suddenly erupted in a thunderous crash, and a cloud of green-black smoke began to billow from the direction of the German trenches.

'Mills bomb,' said Bert.

'Bert,' grunted Ellis, 'you have a wonderful way of stating the obvious.'

Bert sniffed and said nothing. From the darkness in front of them came shouts and screams. A pistol shot rang out and Danny heard the unmistakeable voice of Sergeant Jenkins. 'Fall back. Everybody out of the trench.'

The next second there were running men flashing past their position. Sergeant Jenkins threw himself down next to Ellis. 'Give us two minutes,' he panted, 'then head back yourselves.' He glanced around. 'Where's Corporal Mitchell?'

Danny stared at the spot where Frank had been lying only a few moments before. Now there was no sign of him. 'Must have got lost in the dark, Sarge,' he said.

Jenkins grunted. 'Really? We'll see about that.' He paused. 'Two minutes, Private Evans. No longer.'

A few heads had begun to appear above the German parapet. Danny and Bert were already firing and the shapes ducked back again. They kept up a steady fire, aiming blindly into the darkness. After a few minutes they decided they had done enough and slipped back in the direction of their own lines. As they did so, a star shell burst overhead and they made the final dash with machine gun bullets kicking up the mud at their heels. Gasping for breath, they fell into the trench.

'All back safely?' asked Ellis, once he had regained his breath.

'One man killed in the German trench,' said Sergeant Jenkins, 'another with a bullet in his leg. We came out of it quite lightly, all things considered.'

'Did you get the prisoner?'

Jenkins nodded. 'We got him. Lieutenant Newman is taking him down to base now.'

He turned and strode away to take care of his wounded man. Danny wiped the mud from his tunic and stared at the Sergeant's retreating back. 'I'd just like to know where the hell Frank got to,' he said.

'I think we should go and find out,' said Ellis. 'He's bound to be around here somewhere.'

They found Frank squatting in the first funk hole, shaking and biting at his lip, trying hard to retain what was left of his shattered dignity. Bert caught him by the front of his uniform tunic and pulled him roughly to his feet. 'So what happened to you?'

Frank stared at them, his eyes weak and watering. His gaze flickered from Bert to Ellis to Danny in desperate appeal. 'I must have missed you in the dark,' he said. 'One minute you were there, the next you'd gone. Sorry, lads.'

They said nothing but stared at him in disgust. Then Bert shook his head and thrust him away. Frank fell back against the mud wall and slipped to the ground. The three friends turned on their heels and went back to their dugout. 'What a waste of space,' sighed Bert. 'A bag of wind, that's all he is.'

'He's worse than that,' said Ellis. 'He's dangerous. He could get us all killed.'

*

They were posted to the Ypres salient and took up position four or five miles behind the famous old market town. All day and all night long they could hear the roar of the guns. The noise seemed to be coming from in front, from behind and all around them. Every time they looked to the east, it seemed as if the whole sky was on fire. Clearly something big was about to happen.

'Whatever it is,' said Ellis, 'we'll be part of it.' He was sitting in the barn that the battalion had commandeered, feet dangling over the edge of the hay loft, notebook in his hand.

'New poem?' Danny asked, nodding at the book.

Ellis held it up for Danny to see.

'Can I hear it?'

'I'll try to translate. Listen:

> Neither his sacrifice
> nor his dear face
> can be forgotten
> though the Germans
> stain their fists of steel
> in his blood.'

He stopped and looked up. 'It's not finished yet. I don't suppose that was an accurate translation either – my English isn't that good.'

'It's better than my Welsh,' Danny said. 'I think the poem's good, very powerful. It's full of emotion but sort of controlled, like. Do you see what I mean? I'm not very good at explaining things like that.'

'No, I understand. I think you're right. It's very different from the poem I entered for the National.'

Ellis swung his legs around and climbed to his feet. He stood, listening to the roar of the guns. 'This seems like a pretty big show coming up – could even be the final push. I wonder how many of us will survive?'

Danny wanted to stop him, to protest, but he knew that Ellis was right. The generals, they said, always worked on a percentage casualty figure though nobody quite knew what it was – twenty, maybe even thirty per cent. They just expected so many troops to die in any assault. That was the way of soldiering, Danny supposed, and people like him and Ellis were nothing if not expendable.

The big assault on the Somme had petered out the previous November. This coming attack would be Field Marshal Haig's latest push for victory and, from the number of troops being thrown into the Ypres sector, it was clear that it was intended to be a serious attempt to break the deadlock.

'What worries me,' said Ellis, 'is that if we can see all these preparations being made, so can Jerry. He's got observation balloons all along the lines and there are aeroplanes over our trenches every single day. He'd have to be daft not to realise something's up.'

Danny thought about his words. If he was right, it did not exactly breed much confidence in the coming attack.

Ellis stared down at his notebook and ran his fingers across the lines of verse. 'I'd like to think that if I don't make it – no, don't say anything – if I don't make it, people will still be able to read my poems. I think it's this type of thing they'll remember.' He stared at Danny.

'You'll come through,' said Danny. 'Remember, you've got to get to the Eisteddfod.'

Ellis's smile was wistful and distant. 'Promise me one thing, Danny? If I can't be there, at the National, for some reason – no, listen, please – if I can't be there, promise me you'll go.' He stared, unseeing, through the barn door.

'Ellis?'

Danny's voice jerked him back to reality and he turned to face his friend. Behind the barn, perhaps half a mile to the west, a battery of 12-pounder field guns suddenly opened fire. The blast of the cannonade was like the crack of doom and the wooden walls of the old barn rattled in protest.

'Promise me,' said Ellis, softly.

For a moment Danny could not reply. His friend's words filled him with fear. Ellis was staring at him, eyes full of pleading.

At last Danny nodded. 'I promise,' he muttered.

'Good, then that's settled. I'll sleep more easily tonight.'

There was a sudden commotion from the yard outside and Bert Phillips came skidding through the barn door. He was followed, as ever, by Tudor.

'We're off to the *estaminet* in the village,' he called. 'There's a whole gang of us going. Anything's better than listening to those damned guns. Want to come?'

'Why not!' said Danny. 'Give us two minutes.'

Chapter Nine

The *estaminet* stood in the main street of Poperinghe. It was little more than a terraced house but it was full of soldiers, all calling for beer and wine. Some of them were eating egg and chips, the only food the place sold – as Bert said, at least it made a change from the never-ending stew served up by the army cooks.

They found themselves a table, ordered wine and settled down for the evening. Several of the men at the other tables were singing a selection of sad sentimental songs: 'Roses of Picardy', 'They'll Never Believe Me', 'There's a Long, Long Trail a-Winding'. Mostly, however, the soldiers just sat, talked and drank their wine. The thought of the coming offensive was too close and could not be pushed away.

'Here, Danny,' said Bert, 'that girl over there seems to have taken a fancy to you.' He pointed to the red-haired daughter of the house, a young girl of sixteen or seventeen who had been gazing at Danny for the past half-hour. Tudor nudged him as, scarlet-faced, the young man tried his best to look serious and ignore her.

'It's no good looking at him, love,' Tudor called. 'He's a married man. Come and sit on my lap instead.'

They dissolved into laughter. The girl was not to be

discouraged and soon she was standing by Danny's side. She bent and spoke rapid French into his ear. Danny tried to pull away.

'What's she saying?' asked Bert.

Danny shrugged. 'Search me. I can't understand a word of it.'

'She's saying that you're too young to fight in this war,' said a tall sergeant on the next table. '*Enfant*, she called you – says you're just a child.'

The table erupted into laughter once again. Tudor reached out and tried to grab the girl around the waist but she slipped easily out of his grasp and disappeared in the direction of the kitchen.

'In ten years' time you'll be glad you look so young,' said the sergeant, going back to his beer.

The kitchen door swung open and the girl came out. She was accompanied by an older woman. Quickly, they crossed the floor and stopped at Danny's side. 'Monsieur,' said the woman, 'my daughter would like me to tell you that she means no disrespect. She has a brother who looks just like you – my youngest son, Philippe. He has been in our army at Verdun for the last two years and we have not seen him in all that time.' She wiped her eye with the corner of her pinafore. 'It is terrible when young men have to fight in this dreadful war. She wishes you well and hopes you will keep safe. That is all she wanted to say.'

Before anyone could speak, the two women turned on their heels and disappeared back into the kitchen. Danny lay back in his chair, thinking of Angharad, until he felt Ellis's hand on his shoulder.

'Do you need some fresh air?'

Out in the street it was quiet, apart from the eternal thunder of the guns in the distance. Slowly they walked down the road. 'War touches everyone,' said Ellis, 'no matter who you are. It's a bloody business.'

The eastern sky was full of flashes and sudden lights. Then the rumble of the guns swelled to a roar before fading away again. 'I wonder why they do that?' said Danny. 'It happens all the time.'

Ellis shrugged. 'Just a trick of sound, like a trick of the light, I suppose. The barrage is pretty constant.'

*

When they got back to the *estaminet*, Frank Mitchell had joined their table. He was unsteady on his feet and clearly very drunk. Quite how he had explained his actions in No man's land during their trench raid they never knew. Whatever he had said must have seemed reasonable to Sergeant Jenkins as he had somehow managed to keep his stripe. But since the incident, his attitude had worsened.

'Well, lookie here,' he slurred as Ellis and Danny entered the bar. 'It's the poet and his partner. Been out together writing verses, have we?'

Ellis shrugged. 'No Frank, we've been out listening to the guns. Best to know what we'll be up against.'

The effect of his words was immediate. It was as if he

had struck Frank on the jaw. The man's mouth worked furiously but no words came out. Even alcohol could not cover his fear. He lurched to his feet. 'Need the khazi,' he said, face chalky-white and eyes misty and wet. He stumbled away, knocking into tables and chairs before lurching out of the back door of the *estaminet.*

'God knows what he's going to be like when we go over the top,' said Tudor. 'I just hope he's nowhere near me.'

They said nothing for a few moments. Then, suddenly, Ellis broke the quiet. 'There's nothing more dangerous than a rabid dog,' he said.

Only later, much later, did Danny understand.

*

Two days afterwards the battalion moved into position for the assault. Just before they marched up to the lines, the High Command wheeled in a tame general to give them a pep talk. 'Standard stuff,' said Sergeant Jenkins. 'Just nod your heads, salute when you're told to and be well-behaved little boys.'

They assembled in a hollow, three-sided square while the general and his red-tabbed staff marched to their position on the open side. The general, old, red-faced and out of breath, climbed onto a small box and stood facing them. He puffed out his chest and stared over the assembled ranks with tired, rheumy eyes. After a moment he cleared his throat and began to speak. 'You men have been chosen to perform an important task. To you has been granted the privilege of making the final thrust against the enemy. Your contribution will be crucial and while some of you may fall, you can be sure that your efforts will not be in vain.'

'Bloody charming,' whispered Bert. 'I bet there'll be no chance of him falling.'

'Only off that flamin' box,' said Tudor.

Sergeant Jenkins fixed them both with a fierce glare and they subsided into silence.

'Don't worry about the enemy,' the general continued. 'You will have heard that he is a strong and courageous fighter. He may well be. But remember this, he will never be the equal of good British steel. Or of British soldiers. And anyway, our artillery will have knocked him out long before you are called into action. The enemy guns will be silenced; his barbed wire will be cut. This time there will be no mistake.'

They gave the old man the customary three cheers, Sergeant Jenkins prodding them into action with sharp fingers and hot breath on their backs. The general seemed pleased and beamed in response.

After he had climbed down and gone off to lunch in a nearby chateau, they piled their large packs and all unwanted gear in the battalion transport wagons.

'All your valuables, lads,' called Jenkins. 'Take nothing you're not prepared to lose. It'll all be waiting for you when you get back.'

Danny bundled up Angharad's letters and stored them securely in his pack. He hated the thought of being parted from them but knew that he could not bear it if they were damaged or destroyed in the coming battle. He checked his equipment – water bottle, bayonet, full ammunition pouches. In the small haversack they had all been detailed to carry he put his emergency rations, his gas cape and a spare pair of socks. He was ready.

They were assigned to be part of the first line of reserve and, as such, spent the night before the attack in the communication trenches, a few hundred yards back from the front line. Loaded down with entrenching gear, they moved to their positions with a mixture of trepidation and excitement. Danny had never seen so many soldiers. They were crammed into the trenches, standing or sitting shoulder to shoulder.

By now the artillery barrage was intense, shells whistling over their heads almost every second as they stood waiting in the trench. The noise was deafening, a piercing wail that bit at their eardrums and reverberated around their skulls. The air shimmered and even the ground beneath their feet shook so that they swayed, giddy and light-headed.

'Know what that sounds like?' said Ellis. 'When you stand under a railway bridge and listen to the trains passing overhead.'

Danny nodded. 'Or iron-wheeled goods-wagons full of coal, taking the curves too fast. I used to listen to them all the time back in Treorchy. You can hear them all over town. You can't mistake the noise of those wagons; it's like thunder in the night.'

'You're a poet,' smiled Ellis wryly.

Occasionally the British barrage was answered by the bark of German guns. The Germans were firing at their artillery and most of the shells passed harmlessly over their trenches. It did not stop them worrying.

'That doesn't sound too clever,' said Bert. 'I thought our artillery was supposed to knock their guns into the middle of next week.'

Sergeant Jenkins appeared and herded them into a damp dugout. It was already crammed with a dozen other men but they squeezed in and sat waiting for the dawn and zero hour. Nobody could sleep. Most of them sat writing last letters or, like Frank Mitchell, staring silently into space. Danny pulled out a sheet of paper and, balancing on his pack, began to write.

'Angharad?' asked Ellis.

Danny nodded, signed his name at the bottom of the page and pushed the letter into an envelope. 'I thought I'd write now, while I can, then drop it off with the orderly clerk before zero hour.'

'I hope you sent her my regards?' said Ellis. He had finished his own letter to his mother some time before and was now sitting with his notebook on his knee.

'I suppose we'll be in a pretty dangerous position,' said Danny, 'once things kick off.'

Ellis nodded. The village of Passchendaele had been a thorn in the side of the British forces for two years – this attack was designed, they were told, to capture the village and then wheel northwards towards Ostend and the Channel. The battalion's objective was Pilckem Ridge, a low escarpment behind the German lines, and their platoon had been made the stronghold party under Sergeant Jenkins. He had called it an honour but most of them failed to appreciate the privilege.

'Pill-boxes,' the Sergeant had said. 'That's what you'll find waiting for you, concrete strongholds full of machine guns.'

'And we've got to attack them?' asked Tudor.

Jenkins grinned at him. 'Our artillery should have knocked them out by the time we get there, you 'orrible little soldier. Holding onto 'em, once we've taken them, that's the problem. And that's where you lot come in.'

They had to dig in, Jenkins explained, when the enemy trenches and pill-boxes had been captured, then hold them against the inevitable German counter-attacks. They all carried entrenching tools and some of them had wooden stakes and wire. Even Frank had been lumbered with a coil of barbed wire. Try as he might, he could find no one willing to take his burden off him.

'A bit of a forlorn hope, you could say,' Ellis said, trying hard to force a grin.

Danny stared at him. He didn't know if his friend was talking about Frank's hapless efforts or the job they were expected to do.

Ellis reached out and squeezed his arm. 'Don't you worry. We've trained hard enough, that's for sure.'

Just after 02.00, NCOs came round with an issue of rum. The men grabbed it eagerly. 'Won't be long now,' said Bert.

'Perhaps the barrage has wiped them all out,' said Tudor. 'Perhaps it'll be a cake-walk. The first wave will be able to just walk into their trenches and we won't be needed.'

Nobody answered him. Then, in a moment of utter clarity, the guns stopped. The bombardment had been going on so long that they had begun to regard the thundering as normal. Now, when the noise suddenly halted, the silence was deafening.

'Listen to that,' said Ellis.

'I can't hear anything,' muttered Bert.

'Exactly. That's the sound of silence.'

From the trenches ahead of them, they heard whistles being blown and then came the sound of shouting. The first wave was going over the top. The guns started again, a creeping barrage that was to move forward one hundred yards every three minutes.

'We need to keep fifty to one hundred yards between us and the shell-bursts,' Sergeant Jenkins explained. 'Better to lose a few men from a short shell-burst than to have shells exploding too far ahead. That way the Jerries will have time to get their machine guns up and be ready for us. We've got to hit them just as they're coming out of those deep dugouts of theirs.'

Danny listened to the noise of the renewed firing. He couldn't have explained why but he found the sound quite comforting.

'Right, you lot!' Sergeant Jenkins had appeared at the dugout door. 'It's our turn. Move up, one at a time.

Lieutenant Newman is waiting in the front line. Do what he tells you.'

Danny's heart was huge in his chest as he moved out of the dugout. He felt Sergeant Jenkins slap him on the back but he remembered no words being spoken. He followed Ellis up the trench to where Lieutenant Newman was waiting, at the point where the two trenches met. His face was ashen and his hand shook when he pointed down the trench. 'Spread out, men, and wait for the order.'

Danny gripped his rifle tightly and lay against the trench wall. The smell of the earth was suddenly reassuring and good. Just above his head, growing out from between the sandbags, he saw the slim shape of a poppy, its blood-red petals strangely bright in the dim light of early morning. How strange, he thought, that something so delicate and fine should grow in a hell-hole like this. For a moment he thought of picking it, plucking it from its bed and sticking it in his buttonhole. Something at the back of his mind told him not to, told him it would be unlucky. And so he left it. He closed his eyes and rested his helmet against the trench wall. He felt strangely tired and knew it would have been easy to just drop off to sleep.

A thin drizzle had begun to fall. It lay on the hessian coverings of the men's helmets and on the mud of the trench wall, making everything glisten like silver. Within minutes the rain had increased to a torrential downpour. Danny shuddered.

'Are you all right?' asked Ellis.

Danny opened his eyes and glanced at his friend. Ellis was staring at him and Danny tried hard to conjure a smile in return. 'I'm fine. Good luck.'

Ellis nodded. Then the whistles blew and they went over the top.

Chapter Ten

Danny was astounded to meet no hail of gunfire or shrapnel when he came up from the trench. Perhaps our artillery has wiped them all out, he thought, and then began to walk forward, following Lieutenant Newman through the gaps that had been cut in their own barbed wire. Behind him and alongside him he saw other men doing exactly the same.

'It's going to be a picnic,' he whispered to himself, 'a walkover.' Ahead of him he saw the huddled shapes of soldiers from the first wave lying on the ground and wondered, briefly, why they were taking shelter when everything seemed to be going so well. Then he realised. The men weren't sheltering; they were dead.

'Spread out,' he heard Lieutenant Newman call. 'Don't bunch!'

There was a sudden ping and Newman dropped to the ground, hands clutching helplessly at the earth. He toppled sideways, mud and dirt running from his palms and eyes staring sightlessly towards the German lines. His helmet had fallen from his head and as Danny passed he saw there was a hole the size of a shilling in his forehead.

'Don't stop,' he heard someone shout. 'Don't worry

about the wounded. Stretcher bearers will take care of them.'

Beyond their wire the land fell away before rising once more towards the ominous shape of their objective, Pilckem Ridge. The rain was now lashing down in fury, as if trying to wash them off the face of the earth, and the ground, churned up by artillery shells, was already a sea of mud. Danny was having difficulty walking, thick coils of slime clamping like glue around his boots and puttees. Before he had gone thirty yards, his lungs felt like lead and he realised he was panting from fear and exhaustion.

Their creeping barrage seemed to be miles away in front of them. Danny could see the shell-bursts and knew that they were too far away to offer any protection. The Germans were shelling them now, huge gouts of mud and stones being flung into the air every time one of the missiles landed. And from away to his right came the deadly drum beat of a machine gun. Around him men were beginning to fall, cut down by flailing shrapnel or by machine-gun fire. He cursed the artillery and the ineptitude of the generals whose planning had brought them all to this.

'Keep going, Danny!' He felt rather than saw Ellis by his side. The others all seemed to have disappeared – Bert and Tudor, even Sergeant Jenkins. He ducked his head as a shell exploded in front of him and huge clods of dirt clattered onto his helmet. Spurts of soil began to kick up as the machine gun began another traverse.

'Down here!' Ellis called. He grabbed Danny's arm

and pulled him into a deep shell hole. Three feet of water lay in the bottom but they ignored it and lay, panting, half in, half out of the mud and filth. 'Seems to me like the whole attack is slowing up,' Ellis said. 'This mud is like glue.'

They lay, regaining their breath, for several minutes. Then Ellis glanced over the rim of the shell hole. 'We're moving again,' he called. 'Ready?'

Danny levered himself to his feet. The water ran like blood off his legs. 'Let's go.'

They pushed on, following the bent backs of other soldiers towards Pilckem Ridge. Floundering in the expanse of mud, they panted and slipped their way forward. Rain fell steadily and a grey mist seemed to have descended across the battlefield.

'Those guns,' Ellis shouted, 'they've turned this place into a quagmire. And they still haven't broken the German lines.'

Rifle bullets began to whistle over their heads. The advancing troops, floundering in mud, were an easy target. To his left Danny saw a man fling up his arms and fall backwards into a shell hole. For a moment he thought it was Bert but quickly realised it was someone he did not know and breathed a sigh of relief. Then he heard the woodpecker wail of another machine gun and, ahead of him, saw the earth leaping like hailstones. 'Down!' he yelled. He and Ellis hit the ground at the same time and quickly buried their heads in their arms.

How the bullets missed them Danny never knew. He

saw the lumps of earth jumping in front of him and closed his eyes as they spattered down onto his head. But then the gun continued its traverse and they leapt to their feet and ran on. A sudden rush of air made Danny stagger and grab at Ellis for support. 'What the hell was that?'

They stared around. Huge clouds of smoke were billowing across the battlefield. Ellis shook his head, wiping away the tears with a grimy hand. 'Smoke shells – our smoke shells. They're supposed to give us protection, not fall in amongst us all.'

The long white clouds of smoke were like cloud trails across No man's land and men milled about in confusion. Suddenly Sergeant Jenkins was there beside them. 'We need to take out that pill-box,' he shouted, pointing towards a low concrete bunker that sat in the path directly ahead of them. 'Grenades, that's what we want. Where the hell are our bombers?'

Bert and Tudor appeared behind him, both of them grinning demonically.

'Right here, Sarge,' said Tudor. He reached into the pouches of his webbing waistcoat and pulled out two Mills bombs.

Jenkins waved them forward. Tudor winked at Danny and, with Bert, moved on towards the pill-box. And then the machine gun began again.

'Get down!' shouted Sergeant Jenkins.

The warning was a second too late. The two bombers would not have heard it anyway. The burst of fire caught Tudor as he ran towards the strongpoint. His body jerked and his legs seemed to suddenly slide out beneath him in the mud as he scrabbled to regain his balance. 'No,' he muttered, clutching at the front of his chest. 'Christ, no.'

Then he toppled slowly into the mud and lay still. Bert stood and stared at the body of his friend, eyes wide and mouth working ineffectually.

'Don't just stand there!' roared Jenkins. 'You can't help him any more. But you can get that bloody pill-box.'

Bert glared at him. Without a word he bent and plucked the Mills bombs out of Tudor's lifeless hands. Then he turned and ran for the German position.

'Give him covering fire,' Jenkins called.

They threw themselves down into the mud and began to fire over Bert's head. Danny watched as he hurled himself against the wall of the pill-box. Out of the field of fire he carefully pulled the pins of the grenades and hurled them through the gun ports. 'Now!' he screamed. 'Come on.'

They leapt to their feet and charged as, ahead of them, two loud crumps told them the grenades had reached their target. When they reached the strongpoint, smoke was pouring out through the doors and windows. The sudden image of steam from a saucepan of boiling potatoes flashed into Danny's mind. It was a ridiculous idea and he shook his head to clear it.

Sergeant Jenkins did not hesitate. He dived into the flanking trench and kicked open the pill-box door. Then he raced inside, bayonet ready. Danny followed him. None of the defenders was alive – the deadly Mills bombs had done their work.

'Well done, everybody,' said Sergeant Jenkins. 'Now we've got to consolidate; we need to hold this position. You can bet the Germans will counter-attack within the hour. The units behind us will jump on to the next strongpoint.'

He grinned and rested his backside against the low window ledge. 'We've done our work for a while. But there'll be more to come, mark my words.' He paused and glared around. 'Anybody seen Corporal Mitchell?'

They shook their heads. Nobody had seen Frank since they had first gone over the top. 'It doesn't matter,' said Jenkins. 'Let's see if either of these machine guns is working.'

There were a dozen men in the pill-box and for the next ten minutes they toiled at the guns. The mechanism of one was damaged beyond repair and Jenkins dumped it unceremoniously out of the door. The other gun was soon in working order. They piled barbed wire around the entrance door and built barricades in the flanking trenches. There was little more that they could do.

'Leave it to me,' Bert said, caressing the barrel of the gun. His voice was hard and unwavering. 'If they come I'll blow them all to hell and back.'

Ellis patted him gently on his back. Nobody spoke about Tudor. For perhaps twenty minutes they waited, nerves jangling, each of them desperate for action but fearful too. Sergeant Jenkins kept watch at the rear window of the pill-box. 'Here they come,' he called at last.

Danny stared out of the window aperture. Grey-coated figures were moving over the shattered field, their steel helmets glistening in the rain. Bert dragged the machine gun to the aperture and began to fire. In short, sharp bursts the gun rattled out its hail of death while Danny and the others kept up a rapid rifle fire. Soon the attackers began to falter.

'That's enough,' the Sergeant said. 'Cease firing.'

Three times the German infantry counter-attacked and each time they were beaten back. The morning wore on and the driving rain finally eased into a thin, unpleasant drizzle. By now casualties inside the pill-box were mounting and ammunition was beginning to run low. Sergeant Jenkins was clearly worried.

'We need to get reinforcements up here. And pretty damned quickly at that,' he said. 'One more attack and I reckon we're done for.' He looked towards Bert and the captured German gun. The floor around his feet was littered with spent cartridge cases. 'How many belts of ammunition left?'

Bert shrugged. 'Three, Sergeant.'

Jenkins bit nervously at his thumbnail, considering his next move. Finally he pulled himself up and addressed Ellis and Danny. 'We'll have to get a message back to base. They need to reinforce us now, within the next half hour, if they want us to hold this position. You two get back and tell the CO how serious the situation is. Then double back here, quick as you can.'

Danny grinned at him and raised his eyebrows. 'Two of us, Sarge? To keep each other company?'

Jenkins sighed. 'In case one of you gets himself shot, you fool. And the chances are one of you probably will.' He paused and half smiled. 'Mind you,' he continued, 'if anyone can get through, it'll be you two. Just do your best, lads.'

They gathered up their rifles and moved to the pill-box door. Bert smiled at them, a sad, strained smile, and raised his hand in farewell. Then he turned back to stare out at the German trenches.

A strange hush had fallen over the battlefield. It was as if both sides were gathering their strength, regrouping and waiting for the moment to start the war again. Keeping low, Danny and Ellis swung away from the pill-box across No man's land. It seemed strange to be heading back in this direction, away from the enemy, but they took no chances, moving quickly and silently from one shell hole to the next.

The landscape was littered with dead and wounded and already stretcher-bearers were beginning to move cautiously around the area. Behind them they could see the dark shapes of German soldiers standing up on the sandbags that protected their second and third lines of trenches.

'I think it's a bit soon to be collecting up the dead,' said Ellis. 'Jerry's about to counter-attack again.'

Even as he spoke, a shell whistled overhead, landing with a crash not fifty yards ahead of them. A machine gun opened up from the enemy lines.

'Look out,' Ellis called and dived for cover.

With a strange, dispassionate calm Danny felt the bullets strike him. It was as if he had been punched hard in the groin and leg and, suddenly, he had no strength in the left side of his body. Slowly, almost theatrically, he collapsed onto the mud. He felt the blood running down his leg and the first thought that came to him was that he was going to die. Then an image of Angharad. How sad, he said to himself, I'll never see her again. Even as the idea flashed into his head, he was astounded at the slow clarity of his thoughts.

'Danny!' Ellis was shaking him by the shoulder. 'Stay calm; I'll get you into cover.'

Danny felt himself pulled across the ground, the mud cold and slimy against his back. Then he was falling, tumbling into a new shell crater, one that still stank of cordite, freshly turned earth and wet wood.

'Right,' Ellis panted. 'We'll be all right here. Let me take a look at you.'

He lay his rifle at Danny's side and, as Danny winced in pain, carefully cut away his trouser leg. Then he glanced up and smiled at his friend. 'You'll do,' he said. 'Three nice holes – a real Blighty wound if ever I saw one.'

He pulled out padding and a dressing from his pack and bandaged the wounds as best he could. He gave Danny two of the morphia tablets they all carried and watched as he swilled them down with water from his bottle. 'That should help with the pain,' he said, and then suddenly began to laugh. 'Those Germans must be awful shots – they missed all the vital bits.'

'Angharad will be pleased,' said Danny, relieved and trying his best to smile.

Ellis took a quick glance at the German trenches. It was time to move. 'You'll be safe enough here – just don't poke your head out over the top of this hole. If you do you're liable to get it blown off! I've got to go on. Once I've delivered the Sergeant's message, I'll come back for you.'

Danny nodded. He didn't like to think of Ellis going on alone but he knew that, in his condition, he would not be able to keep up. Ellis was making good sense.

And then, like a vision from a nightmare, he saw Frank Mitchell suddenly appear over the lip of the shell hole. Mitchell was dishevelled and dirty and he had lost his helmet. Yet he still carried his rifle and, strangely, the coil of barbed wire he had been given the night before the attack. His eyes were wild with terror.

Ellis saw Frank at the same moment and rose, slowly, to his feet. He saw the madness in the man's eyes. 'Don't think about it, Mitchell,' he said.

Frank's rifle was already pointing down at Ellis's chest and Danny sensed that he would not hesitate to use it. He felt panic claw at his insides, only too well aware that in this mood Mitchell was capable of anything. Ellis straightened up and backed away, carefully positioning himself between Frank and Danny. 'Where've you been, Frank?' he asked.

Frank grinned. There was no humour in the expression. 'Keeping my head down,' he said. He glanced around, as if watching for some hidden listener, and stared slyly over the lip of the crater. 'It's all too dangerous for me. People are getting killed out there.' He turned back to watch Ellis. 'Just like they are here. Time for a reckoning, poet. I've hated you for too long now – always so clever and so full of yourself, always trying to put me down.' He laughed, manically, waving his rifle in Ellis's face and Danny knew that fear and terror had done their work. Frank had finally slipped over the edge into insanity.

'Like the song says, this is the end of the trail. Leastways, for you. Just one squeeze of this trigger and it's all over. And nobody'll know if it was a British bullet or a German one.' He wiped away a rim of sweat from his upper lip. 'Do you know how good this feels? To have you at my mercy? No, I don't suppose you do. You've probably never felt anger like mine. But you'll regret the day you ever crossed my path. This is it, the end of the line, poet. I'm calling it all in.'

He glanced across Ellis's shoulder. 'I just want you to know that once you're gone, your little friend is next. Can't have any witnesses, can we?'

It was clear that the man was serious. This was not play-acting; he had murder in mind. Panic choking at his throat, Danny's hand snaked out for Ellis's rifle. Frank saw the movement from the corner of his eye and swung around to face the danger.

Fumbling, Danny felt for the trigger but before his fingers could close upon it, Frank had already concertinaed to his knees, and toppled forward into the shell hole, dead before he hit the ground. An unseen German bullet had found its mark.

'Stop, Danny!' gasped Ellis. 'Put the gun down. He's already dead.'

'He was going to kill you,' Danny said. 'He was mad.'

Ellis nodded. He bent and gently took the rifle out of Danny's hands. 'You wouldn't have been able to do it, you know.' He stared down at Frank's body and sighed.

For a long moment neither of them spoke. Then, at last, Ellis turned and jerked his head in the direction of the German lines. 'Look, it all seems to have gone quiet again. If I help you, do you think you can make it back to our trenches? I don't like the thought of leaving you here with that.' He looked across at Frank's body. Danny did not reply but levered himself to his feet. Using Ellis's rifle as a crutch, he limped across the shell hole and glanced quickly over the top. As Ellis had said, everything had gone still and silent, another of those strange, disconcerting lulls that seemed to regularly punctuate the roar of battle.

'You're not the only one,' said Danny. 'Let's get going while we can.' Without looking back, they scrambled out over the rim and set off towards their lines. Each step sent a searing knife of agony through Danny's thigh but he bit hard on his lip and limped on. After a while the firing started again. Machine-gun bullets began to kick up the earth and, glancing back to the German defences, Danny saw grey-coated men standing in front of their trenches, seemingly immune and firing their rifles at anything that moved.

'We'd better get you into cover for a bit,' said Ellis, nodding towards a shallow shell hole. 'We'll wait until this lot eases off.' He helped Danny to the lip of the crater, eased the rifle from his grasp and laid it on the ground. Carefully he lowered Danny down the face of the shell hole, then turned to pick up his rifle.

'Move over, soldier,' he grinned, 'I'm . . .'

There was a sudden bang, strangely loud and definite amongst the din of battle, and Ellis pitched forward. A small gasp, a tiny exhalation of air, escaped his lips and he lay, unmoving, on his face.

'Ellis!' Danny screamed. Ignoring the pain, he dragged himself to the side of his fallen friend. 'Ellis? Speak to me.'

Ellis was conscious but it was obvious, at first glance, that the wound was serious. The bullet had hit him in the back and, struggling to turn him over, Danny immediately saw the blood of the exit wound. He cradled his head and tried so hard not to cry. Ellis lay quietly, looking down at the wound, then smiled weakly. 'That was stupid, wasn't it?' he said as Danny began, desperately, to try to staunch the bleeding.

'Don't talk; you need your strength.'

Ellis shook his head. 'I don't think I'm going to make it, do you? Keeping up my strength doesn't really matter any more.'

Danny buried his head, not able to speak. A huge sorrow gripped him. He knew that Ellis spoke the truth.

'I'm all right, Danny,' Ellis whispered, trying hard to smile for his friend. 'You're safe. I told Angharad I'd keep you safe.' He fell silent and Danny sat quietly by his side. He could not rid himself of a terrible thought – if Ellis hadn't been helping him, he'd have been all right.

As if he could read Danny's mind, Ellis shook his head. 'It's not your fault.'

Danny could not reply. He did not know what to do, what to say or what to think. How long they crouched there he never knew but eventually a sudden movement above the far lip of the crater brought his head around and made him sit up with a start. Pain lanced through his leg and he shouted out in agony, the sound of his cry echoing around the shell hole. The faces of four men, stretcher-bearers, appeared at the lip.

'We've got a live one here, Fred,' one of them called.

Hope surged through Danny's chest. There was a slithering of feet on the mud and stones and within seconds the stretcher-bearers were alongside him.

'My friend,' he managed to gasp. 'My friend first.'

One glance was enough to convince the medics there was nothing they could do for Ellis. But Danny would not let go of hope. 'Tell me he's going to be all right,' he pleaded.

The corporal in charge stared at Ellis, long and hard, then turned to Danny and shook his head. 'I don't think so, son.'

Danny felt the terror in his bowels. It couldn't be true. He and Ellis had shared so much together; it couldn't end like this. He bowed his head and cried, huge sobs that racked his body and tore at the wounds in his leg. Then he felt a hand on his arm.

'Don't worry about me, Danny,' said Ellis, his voice faint and blood beginning to bubble in his lungs. 'I'm really very happy.'

Danny stared at him.

Ellis's eyes fluttered, opened and closed once more. This time they did not reopen. He had already slipped away to some other place, some other consciousness. And Danny knew that, wherever he was, he could not reach him. He watched as two stretcher-bearers lifted him gently onto a stretcher and headed off towards the casualty station.

'Come on, son,' said the corporal. 'Let's get you to safety.'

They limped away out of the shell hole. Danny was conscious of a terrible loneliness. It consumed him and the whole battlefield, the tragic mass of wounded and dying men. And then the shelling began again.

Chapter Eleven

Danny finished his story and sat back in the chair. His cup lay on the table in front of him, the tea untouched and stone cold. He felt as if a huge weight had been lifted from his heart. Thomas Lloyd stared at him, amazement written across his broad, homely face.

'So this corporal of yours, Frank Mitchell, he was going to kill you and kill Hedd Wyn?' he whispered. 'I can hardly believe it. Good God, he was going to kill his own side.'

Danny nodded and looked up earnestly into Lloyd's eyes. 'I would have killed him, you know. I was spared that by a sniper's bullet. We all knew what Frank was like. We should have seen it coming, Ellis, me, Sergeant Jenkins, any of us. But there's no use in thinking like that.' He spread his arms.

For perhaps three minutes neither of them spoke. Lloyd fiddled with his teaspoon, staring around the empty café. 'It's an incredible story,' he said. 'But it's one that can't be told – not for a good many years. That empty chair – the Black Chair – is going to become part of Welsh history. We need that story, the story of Hedd Wyn and his poetry. And his life and courage, come to that. We don't need the truth about Frank Mitchell.'

Danny shrugged. 'Ellis won his Chair – or I should say Hedd Wyn won his Chair. That's all that matters to me. He won't be forgotten; his name will live on.'

'Oh, it will live on, boy; you can be sure about that.' He stopped and reached out to lay his hand on Danny's arm. 'On the battlefield all sorts of things happen. I learned that in South Africa. And on the battlefield legends are born. This story is the stuff of legend. It's safe with me, Danny.'

Danny smiled, knowing the man spoke honestly, knowing he would keep their story for as long as he lived. 'Thank you,' he said.

'But what about the others?' said Lloyd, suddenly. 'Bert and Sergeant Jenkins? And the men in the pill-box? What happened to them?'

'I don't really know,' Danny shrugged. 'Oh, Jenkins got back – of course he did. He's a survivor – backbone of the army, people like him. They had to pull out, retreat from that stronghold, and Sergeant Jenkins led them out. He came to see me in hospital – it seems they're putting him in for a commission. I don't think he likes the idea much but he'll do what he's ordered. He's that type of man.'

'And Bert?'

Danny shook his head. 'I'm not sure. When they pulled out, he refused to go. The last anyone saw of him, he was charging the German rear trenches but what happened to him after that is anybody's guess. He could have been killed or taken prisoner. I just don't know – maybe, after the war, we'll get to find out.'

The bell on the café door jangled harshly behind them and Lloyd turned round in his seat. A girl, a beautiful girl, came into the room and approached their table. Even before Danny spoke, Lloyd knew who it was.

'This is my wife,' Danny said.

Lloyd rose to his feet and held out his hand. 'So you're Angharad.'

The girl smiled at him. 'I've come to take Danny home,' she said. 'I thought I'd find him here.'

Danny pulled himself to his feet while Thomas Lloyd retrieved his crutches from beneath the table. Together they walked to the door and went out onto the pavement, where shadows were already starting to lengthen.

'Back to Treorchy?' asked Lloyd.

Danny shook his head. 'Not yet. We've got one more call to make before we head back south.'

Lloyd nodded.

'I have to see Ellis's mother,' said Danny. 'One last time. I need to see her and tell her how her son died.'

Angharad squeezed Danny's arm, silently, as together they turned and walked away down the street. Thomas Lloyd watched them go.

*

'So what now?' asked Angharad.

'Before Trawsfynydd? Or after?'

'After.'

Danny shrugged. He had not really thought about it.

His wounds would keep him out of the war – he knew his soldiering days were over. But what to do with the rest of his life? He had lived from one day to the next for so long now that to think of long-term plans did not come easily. Angharad smiled and linked her arm through his.

'There's a smallholding available, up on the mountain above Caerphilly – nothing big, just a hundred acres or so. It's the ideal place to raise a few cattle and grow some crops – at least that's what the land agent said.'

Danny stared at her. 'How do you know all this?'

'I've been keeping my eyes open and I went to see the agent last week, before you came out of hospital.' She smiled at him and squeezed his arm tightly. 'You always said you'd like to try farming. If you want it, Danny, the lease can be ours. You've only got to say the word.'

Danny felt salt tears stinging at the corners of his eyes.

'Oh, Danny,' she whispered, 'this is what Ellis would have wanted for you. You know that, don't you?'

He finally managed to find the words. 'I know. It's exactly what he'd have chosen. As Sergeant Jenkins would say, I seem to have been outflanked.' And then he paused, gazing down at Angharad.

'Annie, you know what you said about cattle? Do you think we could find room for a few sheep, too? I have a hankering to raise some sheep.'

Afterword

This book does not claim to be an accurate historical account of the life and death of the poet Hedd Wyn – Ellis Humphrey Evans. It is a work of fiction, a novel that tries to tell the story of men and women during one of the most dramatic and dreadful wars in history, the Great War of 1914–1918. Hedd Wyn appears as one of the main characters, just one of thousands of young men caught up in the struggle.

I have tried to be as true to Hedd Wyn's story as is possible, as far as it is known, but I have interpreted his character as I have seen fit – there is nothing to say that the real man was or was not like the fictional character in the book. Other characters such as Danny and Angharad, Sergeant Jenkins and Bert Phillips are entirely products of my imagination although there are enough surviving records and first-hand accounts to indicate that there were thousands of people just like them living through that traumatic period.

Facts about Hedd Wyn's death are hard to uncover, as you might expect in the chaos of a battle like Passchendaele – or Third Ypres as it is more correctly known. My description of his death is purely fictional. Other events, like Hedd Wyn being granted leave of absence from the army to help with the family ploughing, the attack on Pilckem Ridge and the awarding of the Chair at the National Eisteddfod, are as close to reality as I can make them.

The final words should, really, belong to Hedd Wyn himself, albeit in translation. They seem, I think, to sum up the quality of the man and his concern for his friends and comrades:

> 'The lads' wild anguish fills the breeze,
> Their blood is mingled with the rain.'

Glossary of Terms

Battalion: an infantry unit made up of three or four companies, part of a regiment.

Blighty wound: soldiers' slang for a wound that was serious enough to have them sent back home to Britain (Blighty).

Boer War: war fought between Britain and the Boer Republics of South Africa, 1899 to 1902.

Brass Hats: soldiers' slang for members of the staff – generals and their advisors – so-called because of the red tabs on their uniform and gold decoration on their hats.

CO: Commanding Officer.

Conscription: the compulsory enlistment of men in the armed forces, introduced in Britain in January 1916.

Dugout: a shelter, sometimes underground, sometimes in the side of a trench.

Estaminet: a French café/bar that sold egg, chips and wine, the favourite food of soldiers during the Great War.

Fire step: a ledge at the front of a trench, where soldiers stood to fire their rifles.

Flanders: part of Belgium where most of the fighting took place during the Great War.

Fritz: soldiers' slang for German troops.

Jerry: soldiers' slang for German troops.

Kaiser:	the German Emperor Wilhelm II. The grandson of Britain's Queen Victoria, he abdicated when Germany lost the war, and went into exile in 1918.
Lee Enfield:	the short-magazine Lee Enfield rifle, the main British infantry weapon of the war.
Litherland:	the main camp and base depot of the Royal Welch Fusiliers.
Mametz Wood:	German-held wood attacked by the 38th Division, the Welsh Division, during the Battle of the Somme in 1916.
Mills bomb:	a British hand grenade, fired once the priming pin was removed, leaving a number of seconds before it exploded so that enemy soldiers could not throw it back.
Minnie:	British name for *minenwerfer*, a German trench mortar.
NCO:	non-commissioned officers such as corporal and sergeant.
No man's land:	the open ground between the rows of British and German trenches.
Over the top:	phrase used to denote taking part in an attack, going over the top of the trench.
Passchendaele:	the name of a village close to Ypres but often used to denote the Third Battle of Ypres, a battle that bogged down in a sea of mud.
Pill-box:	a strongpoint, usually built of concrete and armed with several machine guns.
Platoon:	a section of an infantry company commanded by a lieutenant.
Puttees:	long strips of cloth wound around the lower leg of soldiers, from ankle to calf.

Royal Welch Fusiliers: a regiment in the British army made up, in the main, of soldiers from Wales and the west Midlands – the name is spelt in the old, traditional manner.

RSM: Regimental Sergeant Major, a senior non-commissioned officer.

Salient: a bulge in the line of defences that projects closest to the enemy.

Sandbags: bags of earth laid in front of and behind trenches to protect soldiers from the blast of artillery shells.

Sam Browne belt: a belt worn by officers, across the chest, to link with another belt around the waist.

Somme: a battle in the Somme area of France, begun on 1 July 1916, which eventually cost over one million British, French and German lives.

Stand To: the term derived from the command 'Stand to your arms.' Every dawn and dusk, troops had to 'Stand To' their battle stations in case of an attack.

Tin town: a name commonly given by British soldiers to any collection of tin huts where they were billeted.

Trenches: deep zigzagging ditches dug by soldiers to provide cover. As the Great War progressed, trenches soon stretched for over 400 miles across Europe. They became living quarters for the troops.

Verdun: the costliest battle ever fought by French armies (1916) defending the fortress town of Verdun.

Western Front: the name given to the lines of trenches in France and Belgium, originally coined by the Germans who were, literally, fighting on their western front.

Zeppelin: a lighter-than-air German airship used to bomb English towns and cities.